**Look for other titles about the
WILD AT HEART vet volunteers:**

ANIMAL RECORD

e

ne

ne Deer

ale

arkings light brown

Breed White-tail

Age 6 mos.

Weight

TREATMENT

Found tangled in barbed wire.
Multiple lacerations.
Sedate. Clean and suture cuts.
Leg x-rays negative
Monitor for shock,
admin. fluids if nec.
TMT: Antibiotic injections daily, release to
Lakes' wildlife rehab. ctr. When stabl

Trapped

Laurie Halse Anderson

Acknowledgments

Special thanks to Ellen Miles. Thanks also to Kimberly Michels, D.V.M.; Trish O'Connell of the Schuylkill Center Wildlife Rehabilitation Clinic in Philadelphia; Richard Peck of the Peck Petting Farm in Spring Green, Wisconsin; and the Sherman family.

Published by Pleasant Company Publications
Text Copyright © 2001 by Laurie Halse Anderson
Illustration and Design Copyright © 2001 by Pleasant Company

Although Ambler, Pennsylvania, is a real town (a wonderful town!), the setting, characters, and events that take place in this book are all fictional. Any similarity to real persons, living or dead, is coincidental and not intended by the author. This book is not intended as a substitute for your veterinarian. Your vet is the best source of health advice for your pet.

Printed in the United States of America.
01 02 03 04 05 06 07 08 RRD 10 9 8 7 6 5 4 3 2 1

American Girl® and Wild at Heart™ are trademarks of Pleasant Company.

Cover Photography: Brian Malloy
Title Page and Newspaper Clipping Photography: Jamie Young
Photo Credits: Title Page—deer closeup: ©2000 Kevin Lammi at Northland Images (www.northlandimages.com); Title Page—deer side-view: ©Buddy Mays/CORBIS; Title Page—landscape: Lara Klipsch; p. 111—©CORBIS; p. 112—©Hulton-Deutsch Collection/CORBIS; p. 113—kittens: ©Dorling Kindersley; p. 113—volunteers: ©Roger Ressmeyer/CORBIS; p. 114—©Joseph Sohm; ChromoSohm Inc./CORBIS.

Library of Congress Cataloging-in-Publication Data
Anderson, Laurie Halse.
Trapped / Laurie Halse Anderson.
p. cm. — (Wild at Heart ; 8)
Brenna, one of the volunteers at the Wild at Heart animal clinic, is horrified to find a dog caught in a trap in the local nature preserve, but subsequent events prove that every story has two sides.
ISBN 1-58485-124-4 (pbk.)
[1. Trapping—Fiction. 2. Dogs—Fiction. 3. Animals—Treatment—Fiction.
4. Veterinarians—Fiction.] I. Title.
PZ7.A54385 Tp 2001   [Fic]—dc2   2001022289

Dedication

In memory of my grandfather, Henry Walton Holcomb

First, I'm a dog. Then I'm a cat. Then a cobra, a frog, and a fish. No, I'm not some nut revisiting my past lives. I'm just doing yoga.

It's Sunday, and Mom and I are in the sunroom. Our house—it's more of a cabin, really—is in the middle of a forest. But somehow, even with all those trees around, this room is always full of sun in the morning. The warm rays find me wherever I move as Mom and I go through each of the postures. I stretch and hold, paying attention to my breath and to how my body feels.

My mom loves yoga because it's relaxing and teaches her to "live in the moment." She thinks it's good for me for those reasons. But I love it because I get to be each animal as I do the postures. Have you ever seen a dog stretching first thing in the morning? Then you already know how to do the

Downward Facing Dog, one of my favorite yoga postures. When I hold that pose, I'm not Brenna Lake anymore. I'm off in some other world.

"Should we finish up with a Lion?" Mom asks.

I grin at her. "Definitely."

"Me, too! Me, too!" My little brother, Jayvee, runs into the sunroom. He's too squirmy to do a whole session of yoga with us, but he loves the Lion pose. So do I.

We kneel facing each other. To do the Lion, you open your eyes really wide. Then you take a deep breath, open your mouth as far as you can, stick your tongue out, and go "Aaaaarrrrrhhh!"—roaring like a lion. Then you crack up, because everybody looks so hilarious.

Mom, Jayvee, and I open wide and give our best roars. Then we all fall over on the soft beige rug, laughing our heads off. I grab Jayvee and give him a big hug. He's still young enough to let me do that, sometimes.

"Well," Mom says, as we sit up and brush ourselves off. "At least we haven't been abandoned by all our boys."

I smile sympathetically as she gives Jayvee a squeeze. Sunday mornings aren't the same lately, and we're both sad about it. Once upon a time, yoga was a family thing. But these days Dad is way too busy with his carpentry (he has a shop next to our house), and my older brother, Sage, has "more important things to do."

Sage is seventeen and Jayvee is seven. They both look almost exactly like my dad, with dark eyes and wavy brown hair, except Dad's the only one with a beard and an earring in one ear.

Sage and I used to be best buds. We hiked in the woods together, rode bikes, and worked in the critter barn with Mom and Dad. My parents are wildlife rehabilitators. Our family takes in and cares for injured wildlife until the animals can be released back into the wild.

But lately Sage and I aren't so close. He spends a lot of time in his room, working on the computer. And he's also been going to meetings of this group he joined called Animals Always. It's a bunch of local animal rights activists who are totally dedicated to their cause. They're very active in this part of Pennsylvania, doing things like picketing stores that sell fur, campaigning against hunting, and writing letters to newspapers about all kinds of animal rights issues.

Sage has become passionate about animal rights. It's all he ever seems to think or talk about.

I love animals, too. I always have. I spend most of my free time working with them, both at home and at Wild at Heart. That's our local veterinary clinic, which is run by a very cool woman named J.J. Mackenzie, otherwise known as Dr. Mac.

I'll be heading over to the clinic later to join my friends Maggie Mackenzie and her cousin Zoe Hopkins (they're Dr. Mac's granddaughters), Sunita Patel, and David Hutchinson. We've all been volunteering at the clinic for a while now.

I've learned so much about animals working with Dr. Mac. I love every minute I spend there, even if I'm not doing anything more exciting than mopping an exam room floor.

So, you'd think Sage and I would have lots to talk about. And we do, as long as I'm willing to listen to him lecture about the terrible way lab monkeys are treated, or why nobody should wear anything made of fur or even leather.

I understand his point. I mean, I can get angry about the way animals are treated, too. I've been known to lose my temper about it, fly off the handle a bit. (I'm working on that!) Mom says I've got to learn that everything isn't always black and white, though I can't see how hurting animals is ever anything but just plain evil. But Sage is going a little overboard with the animal rights thing, and I kind of miss the old days when we could just have a normal conversation.

I think Mom's a little worried about Sage, too. Animals Always members have been known to get themselves arrested or hurt just to get attention for their cause. I think Mom and Dad both have their fingers crossed that Sage will stay out of trouble. I know I do.

"Want to help me in the critter barn?" Mom asks as we roll up our purple yoga mats.

"Sure. Then can we make waffles?"

"Absolutely!" Mom smiles at me.

"Yay, waffles!" Jayvee jumps up and down. "I'll tell Dad and Sage." He runs off on his errand.

As we leave the house, Poe flaps and caws at me. "OK, pal, you can come," I tell him, bending toward his perch. He hops onto my shoulder and gives me a little nibble on the ear.

Poe is my pet crow. His full name is actually Edgar Allan Poe. He was shot by a hunter and we rehabbed him, but his wing was ruined forever. Since he'll never fly again, my folks let me keep him. But Poe is way more than a pet. Sometimes I think he may be the best friend I ever had. He loves to make me laugh, he listens to everything I tell him without judging, and he's always there when I need him. What more do you want in a friend?

Mom and I work quickly in the critter barn, making sure that all our current "guests" have been fed and that their cages or tanks are clean.

Sage surprises me by turning up to join us as we're doing our rounds. "Haven't seen the critters in a couple of days," he mutters, stealing some lettuce from my basket to give to one of the turtles.

At the moment, we're caring for a sick raccoon, an owl with a broken wing, and two injured turtles someone found on the side of the road. I stick Poe into an empty bird cage while I work, since owls are crows' worst enemies. I don't need Poe—or the owl—getting all riled up.

Seeing the turtles makes me so mad. Whoever hit them didn't even stop the car! One of the turtles may be blind for life; the other one has a partially crushed shell and a broken foot. I grumble about how unfair it is that they were hurt.

"Honey, it can be hard to see something that small when you're driving," my mother reminds me. She's carrying an armload of hay to the raccoon's cage.

"Well, then, maybe some people shouldn't have cars in the first place!" I say.

Mom gets that look on her face. She thinks I'm doing that "black and white" thing again. Maybe I am. But I'm right. People should learn to get along without cars. There would be a lot fewer accidents, less pollution, and NO roadkill.

Sage agrees with me. "Maybe somebody should throw some tacks on the road at strategic places," he suggests, grinning a little to show that he's just kidding. (Or is he?) "Maybe that would slow those drivers down. There's no excuse for killing animals." Now he's not grinning anymore. He's as mad as I am, maybe even angrier.

Mom just shakes her head.

I haven't cooled down by the time we close up the barn. Poe always hates it when I get upset. So, instead of hopping onto my shoulder, he chooses to ride with Mom. I pretend not to care.

We stop by the carpentry shop to let Dad know that brunch will be ready soon. He's sanding some long planks, but when he sees us, he turns off the noisy machine for a minute.

"Jayvee already informed me that we're having waffles." He grins as he wipes his forehead with a dirty red bandanna. "Sounds great! I'm starved."

No wonder. He's working so hard! The shop is full of sawdust, and it looks much messier than usual. Normally, every tool is in its place and the shop is clean and tidy. But Dad just hasn't been able to keep up with his orders lately. That's a good thing for the family bank account but not such a good thing for Dad.

"Sage, I could really use your help in here this afternoon," he says.

Sage just shakes his head. "Got a meeting," he mumbles. He doesn't meet Dad's eyes.

Dad sighs. "You know . . ." he begins.

Sage holds up a hand. "I know, I know. You're working hard to save money for my college education. Well, I never asked you to!"

My brother has been threatening not to go to college next year. He says it's a waste of time and he wants to do something more "proactive," whatever that means.

Dad starts to answer, but Mom puts a hand on his arm. "We'll talk about it later," she says. "Why don't you clean up? Waffles will be ready in ten minutes."

Sage disappears upstairs as soon as we get back in the house.

Mom and I work together in the kitchen, making the batter for waffles and cutting up fresh fruit for a topping. Jayvee tries to help, too, but mostly he gets in the way.

Just when I'm sure that I'm going to faint from hunger, brunch is ready. Dad comes in and washes up, but we have to call Sage three times before he hears us. When he's on the Internet, he tunes everything else out.

"Smells delicious!" Dad says as we sit down around the small kitchen table. It's a tight fit, but I like being cozy. We clasp hands. Dad squeezes my hand, and I pass the squeeze along to Jayvee. He passes it to Mom, who passes it to Sage, who passes it back to my dad. The squeeze goes around and around, faster and faster, until we're all squeezing at once. Then it's time to eat.

Dad spoons a big pile of strawberries and bananas onto his waffle and takes a huge bite. "Mmmm," he says. "Spectacular!"

The rest of us dig in, too. Except for Sage.

He just sits there, looking down at his plate. "Are there eggs in here?" he asks, poking at his waffle, which is rapidly growing cold.

Mom sighs. "Two. Is that a problem?"

Sage pushes his plate away. "I guess I forgot to tell you," he says. "I decided to go vegan."

Wow. That's big news. Vegans are sort of like ultra-vegetarians. They don't eat meat or any other animal products, like milk or eggs or cheese. Vegans don't wear leather, and some of them won't even eat honey because they believe it's unfair to the bees to steal what they've created.

"Oh, Sage," Mom says. "Don't you think—"

"I do think," he says, interrupting her. "I think about the appalling conditions that the chickens who lay those eggs live in. It's barbaric to force animals to live that way! I won't be a part of that kind of exploitation." He shoves his chair back from the table. "I don't know how the rest of you can live with yourselves," he adds angrily. Then he stomps out of the room and back up the stairs.

The kitchen is silent. We just sit there, stunned.

I've lost my appetite.

TWO

So, brunch is basically a total bust. Nobody talks much after Sage's outburst. He may have left the room, but the tension hasn't. Silently, we finish our waffles. Then Dad pushes his chair back and carries his plate to the sink. I help clear the table without being asked.

"Want a ride to Dr. Mac's?" my mom asks as she wipes down a counter. "I'm due at work in an hour. I can drop you off on the way."

Mom works at the local retirement home, Golden Age. The old people over there love her, because she's always so upbeat. She'll have to fake it today, though. I can tell she's pretty upset about Sage.

"Thanks, but I think I'll go for a walk," I tell her. "I'll bike over later."

I need some time in the woods. That's where I go to relax, to think.

"OK." She smiles. "Oh, if you go to the creek, try to find some crayfish for the raccoon. And the turtles would love some—"

"Mushrooms," I say. "I know. I'll bring a basket."

I get a basket and my jacket. I grab my camera, too. On my way out the door, Poe flaps and caws for attention. "Not this time, pal," I tell him. I want to take some pictures, and he scares off the wildlife by cawing at the worst moments. To make up for not bringing him along, I offer Poe a couple kernels of popcorn, one of his favorite treats. He knows I'm buying him off, but his stomach gets the better of him, and he gobbles them down.

"Bye, Mom," I say. Dad's already back in the shop, and Jayvee's playing in the sunroom. Sage is up in his room, of course.

Mom gives me a quick hug. "Bye, honey." She brushes back a strand of my brown hair, just like hers only without the gray, and looks into my eyes. Then she says, "Why don't you see if Sage wants to go along? He could use some fresh air."

I want to tell Mom not to worry about him, but how can I? I'm worried, too. "Good idea," I say.

I kiss Mom on the cheek and take the stairs two at a time to Sage's room. I poke my head in, but he's focused on the computer screen. He doesn't hear me clear my throat, or maybe he does and decides to ignore me.

I don't stick around to find out.

I leave through the back door and set out on the path behind our house. There's a whole network of trails through the nature preserve that surrounds our cabin, so I can take a different walk every day of the week. This time, I head toward the creek. There's something about the sparkling clear water splashing over the mossy stones that helps to clear my head. When I'm upset, I go sit by the water and listen to it, and I always leave feeling better.

I'm never bored in the woods, because the woods are always changing, depending on the season, the weather, and even the time of day. Right now, all the leaves are turning orange and gold and brown. The fallen ones rustle beneath my feet as I walk along, and I can smell their earthy scent. I pick up a few of the prettiest ones and put them in my basket. I'll press them between wax paper to make decorations for our windows.

Sage and I camped out here last summer, watching the stars shine through the pine boughs as we stayed up talking. We traded stories about school, and he told me what things were like when he was my age. Like how he declared himself a "pacifist" in sixth grade and got teased mercilessly. A bully named Steven Bauer made it hard for Sage to stick to his principles, but Sage never took the bait. I was proud of my big brother for that.

I wonder if Sage would be able to put up with someone like Steven Bauer today. Sage seems so angry and obsessed lately. If we camped out now, he would probably just lecture me for hours.

I take a deep yoga-breath and let it out. *Think calm. Think peaceful.* I grab my camera and look up at the trees through the viewfinder. Their tall trunks rise into the sky majestically. I know they're just trees, but somehow they look old and wise.

I try to imagine how the shot will look in black and white. That's the type of film I usually use. It's the best way to capture the lights and darks of the forest. You can really see the details of something when you don't have color to distract you. You see what's true. Of course, that might just be me being "black and white" again!

Somehow I don't feel like clicking the shutter just now. I let the camera drop to my side and stand still for a moment, to soak it all in.

It's so quiet, I can hear a woodpecker drumming away on a dead tree and two chickadees calling to each other.

Suddenly I hear another sound, a crashing noise coming from my right. I look over just in time to see a young deer leaping through the underbrush. Its white tail flashes as it bounds away, faster than I could ever run. I must have scared the animal when I moved. I wish I could call out to it, tell it that it's safe here in the nature preserve.

And I would have loved to snap the deer's picture, but it was moving way too fast for that.

I walk down to the creek now and stoop to take a closer look at a tiny fern growing out of a rock. Mom and I are trying to learn to identify the different types, but I can't remember what this one is called. I take out my camera again and focus on the fern. *Click*. I'll look it up in our field guide when I get my pictures back.

As I straighten up, I hear something else. A whimpering sound, very faint. I know that sound.

It's an animal in pain.

I listen carefully to figure out which direction it's coming from, then tuck my camera into my basket and start to run.

I come into a clearing just beyond the creek, near an old apple tree that still blooms sometimes in the spring. The whimpering sound is louder here, but I can't tell what it is.

Then I look down near the base of the tree, and I gasp.

There's a wolf lying there.

No. That can't be!

There are no wolves in these woods. I take a closer look. It's a dog, but the shape of his head and his thick, shaggy coat make him look like a wolf.

This dog is in trouble. His beautiful coat—shades of cream, tan, and gray tipped with brown—is dull and matted. And he's so thin I can practically count every rib. I can see the way his panting makes his chest rise.

At least he's still alive.

I approach him carefully, trying to see if he's wearing a collar.

"Are you OK, boy? What happened?"

He watches me closely and curls his upper lip, but he's too exhausted to growl, much less snap at me. He can barely lift his head. I can't figure it out. Why is he just lying there?

Then I take one step closer, and I know.

My stomach flips over. My knees turn to Jell-O. Suddenly I can't catch my breath.

The dog's front leg is caught in a trap.

THREE

I can't move. I just stand there, staring at the dog. "Oh!" is all I can say. "Oh, no!"

He looks up at me. His brown eyes are dull.

I pull it together. "Wait here, boy," I tell the dog. "I'll be right back." I want to stroke his fur, to comfort him, but I know better than to touch an animal in distress.

I turn and start running. It isn't easy, because my eyes are filled with tears, but I thread my way through the trees and take a shortcut back to the house.

I make it back in record time and burst into Dad's carpentry shop. He looks up, startled.

"Brenna?" he asks. He puts down the piece of wood he's holding, turns off the saw, and comes toward me, taking off his safety goggles. "What is it, honey?"

"It's a dog!" I say. "His foot is in a trap. I think he's—" I take a huge, sobbing breath, "—dying."

Dad doesn't waste any time. He steps to the door of his shop. "Jayvee!" he yells. Jayvee is playing out back. "Tell Sage to call Dr. Mac's. We're bringing in an emergency patient. Then call Mrs. Piper and ask if you can go play with Jason for a while." He turns back to me. "Let's see," he says. "We'll need a chain cutter to get the trap off. And a first-aid kit, and probably a litter to transport the poor guy . . . Gloves . . . Something to muzzle him with."

He's thinking out loud. He walks through the shop, grabbing things and handing them to me. Then we head over to the critter barn to get some more supplies. Sage meets us there.

"What's up?" he asks. "I called Dr. Mac. She'll be ready when we get there."

"Dog in a trap," Dad says.

Sage curses.

Dad doesn't even blink at the swearword. "Come with us," Dad says. "We may need help carrying the animal."

Our neighbor, Mrs. Piper, comes to pick up Jayvee, and we take off. As we head back down the path into the woods, I look at Sage, trotting next to me. His mouth is a tight line and his eyes are dark and intense. I barely recognize him. He's not saying a word, but he doesn't have to. I know what he's thinking. He is furious.

So am I. How could someone hurt an innocent animal that way? I picture the dog running along, nose to the ground and tail wagging, happy and free. Then I imagine the sickening snap of the trap, the metal jaw springing closed and clamping around his leg, and the fear the dog must have felt when he realized he was caught. Ugh. I shake my head to clear the image away and concentrate on leading Dad and Sage to the dog.

When we come into the clearing, the dog doesn't even move. His eyes are open and he's still panting, but he has no energy left to react. Sage squats down and shakes his head in disgust.

Dad moves slowly, gently. He talks to the dog in a low voice as he pulls on his gloves. Quickly, Dad wraps a soft piece of gauze around the dog's muzzle. That will keep the dog from biting. Then Dad reaches for the chain cutter and slices right through the chain that holds the trap to an anchor buried in the dirt.

"We'll take that off at Dr. Mac's," Dad says, sighing at the mess the trap has made of the dog's foot.

I don't look too closely, but what I do see turns

my stomach. The wound around the trap is raw, and I think I can see bone.

"Let's lift him onto the litter," Dad says to Sage.

The litter is a piece of canvas slung between two wooden rods. Dad and Sage get in position, one on either side of the dog. I stand by. "On my count," Dad says. "One, two, three." They lift, I move the litter beneath the dog, and we're ready to go.

Dad and Sage carry the litter and I walk behind, carrying the chain cutter and first-aid kit. We're moving more slowly now, since they have to be careful not to jostle the dog. It seems to take hours to get back to the house, even though it's really only minutes.

I open the gate of Dad's pickup, and Dad and Sage ease the litter into the truck bed. I hop in next to the litter while the two of them get into the front seats. I'm not usually allowed to ride in back, but this time Dad doesn't try to stop me. He starts up the truck and takes off. We've barely spoken a word.

I study the dog lying next to me. His eyes are glazed, and he's panting harder than ever. I check the second hand of my watch and try to count his respirations, his breaths. Dr. Mac will need that information. But the road is bumpy and I can't concentrate. And I know better than to reach over and take his pulse, even though he's muzzled. I don't want to make him any more stressed than he is.

He's wearing a worn leather collar. It has no tags that I can see, but the collar means he must once have been somebody's pet, even if he's a stray now.

I talk to him in what I hope is a low, soothing voice like the one Dad was using, but I can't hide how upset and angry I am. "It's gonna be OK, boy," I say, even though I'm not so sure.

He needs a name. I can't just keep calling him "boy." We don't usually name the animals we rehab, but this case is different. "Chico," I say softly. That means *boy* in Spanish. The dog's left eyelid twitches. "Chico," I repeat. "That's your name. Listen, Chico, we're going to do everything we can to help you. Dr. Mac is the best vet in the world."

I shout to Dad through the little window between the pickup bed and the cab. "How long do you think he was in that trap?" I ask.

I see Dad's eyes in the rearview mirror. He looks tired, sad. There are little bits of sawdust in his beard. "Almost too long," he shouts back, shaking his head. "It looks like he may have tried to chew off his own foot to escape."

I hear Sage swear again. This time Dad shoots him a look. "That's enough," he says.

"Enough?" Sage asks. "What, so I'm supposed to sit here politely while some idiot is torturing animals?" He folds his arms across his chest. "OK," he says. "I'll keep my mouth shut. Actions speak louder than words, anyway."

Dad looks over at him. "What exactly do you mean by that, Sage?" he asks.

Sage just shakes his head, refusing to speak.

"Sage." There's a warning in Dad's voice.

Sage looks out the window, his mouth set in that hard line.

I turn back to Chico. "It's gonna be OK," I tell him again. "We'll take care of you."

✚

Maggie runs out as soon as we pull into the clinic parking lot. "What's going on?" she asks. Sunita, David, and Zoe are right behind her.

"It's a dog," I explain. "He got caught in a trap."

I hear gasps, then questions, but I'm too distracted to tell them any more. Dad and Sage are guiding the litter out of the truck.

"Oh, man," Maggie groans when she sees Chico. "That dog is in trouble." She runs into the clinic to let her grandmother know that we're here.

Zoe holds the door for us. Sunita and David just

watch the litter go by, shaking their heads.

"That's awful," Sunita says. "Aren't those traps illegal?"

We follow Maggie past the reception area and beyond the two exam rooms, right into the operating room. Dr. Mac has prepped the stainless steel table by disinfecting it and putting down a warm pad covered with an old towel. The pad, called a water blanket, is heated with hot water and helps stabilize animals who might be going into shock.

Dr. Mac asks Maggie, Sunita, and David to go back to their regular Sunday jobs, cleaning the reception area and the exam rooms. "Brenna, you can stay in here and help," she tells me.

Dad and Sage gently lift Chico off the litter and onto the table. He doesn't even seem to notice or care where he is.

Frowning as she gazes down at the injured dog, Dr. Mac runs a hand through her short gray hair. "I guess I won't need to sedate him," she says.

"He's pretty out of it," Dad agrees.

"But let's get a real muzzle on him, just to be safe," Dr. Mac continues. Then she looks at me. "You found him?" she asks.

I nod.

"We'll do everything we can," she tells me.

"I know," I say. "That's what I've been telling him. I've been calling him Chico."

"Chico?" she asks. She looks at him again and pushes up her sleeves. "OK, Chico," she says. "Let's get a temperature, pulse, and respirations." She works quickly and efficiently, touching Chico gently. She reels off the numbers, and I scribble them down on a clinic record sheet.

Dr. Mac runs her hands all over Chico's body, checking for injuries. "Hmmm, he's definitely malnourished," she says, as she feels his ribs. She takes a gentle pinch of his skin, lets go, and watches to see how long it takes the pinched part to spring back to normal. "Dehydrated, too. Brenna, can you grab an I.V. bag of Lactated Ringer's? We'll get him started on that right away."

I get a bag from the cupboard and hang it on a metal stand, the way we've learned. Dr. Mac connects some plastic tubing to the bag. Then she inserts an I.V. catheter into Chico's left rear leg. "Normally, I'd want to put this in a foreleg," she says, "but it might be in our way."

After she gets the I.V. going, she prepares a couple of injections. "Antibiotics," she says, as she gives Chico a shot. "And some steroids for shock. I'll give him pain medication, too."

"What about a rabies shot?" I ask. "In case he hasn't had one recently." There's no way to tell, since he doesn't have any tags on his collar.

Dr. Mac shakes her head. "We can't give him a rabies shot, or any other vaccinations, until he's recovered. We don't want to put any more stress on his immune system. For now, we'll just have to be careful when we handle him."

Chico is still lying there quietly. The only movement that I can see is in his ribcage. He's panting a little bit.

"OK, let's get this thing off," Dr. Mac says, making a face at the trap. "If you two can help . . ." She looks at my dad and Sage. "I'll hold Chico and stabilize the leg while you pry the jaws apart."

Dad and Sage step forward. I can't see exactly how they do it, but in a minute the trap is off and Dr. Mac is looking at Chico's leg.

"Badly damaged," she says, shaking her head. "That trap's been on for a while, and it's cut right through some muscles and tendons. The bone may even be fractured, and there's probably nerve damage." She flushes the wound with sterile saline solution so she can see it better.

"But you can fix it, right?" I ask.

For a second, she doesn't answer. She's applying

some ointment to the wounds, and she doesn't look up at me.

"Dr. Mac?" I need to know.

"I'm not sure, Brenna," she tells me, meeting my eyes. "The tissue beneath the area where the trap was may be dead, beyond saving. If it is, it could become gangrenous, and that kind of infection could kill Chico."

"So, what are you saying?" I hold my breath.

"We have to get him stabilized first, no matter what. Tomorrow, I'll take another look at the wound and see how it's doing. If there's any blood still moving through the foot, we may be able to save it." She pauses and looks down at Chico. "But there's a good chance I'll have to amputate."

Sage shakes his head in disgust. "If that dog loses its leg—" he begins, like he's going to make some kind of threat.

Dad shushes him. "Not now, Sage."

I see Dr. Mac's eyes go from Dad to Sage. She knows my family pretty well, and she can tell when there's trouble between us. But I can't think about the tension between my dad and Sage right now. I'm trying to make sense of what Dr. Mac just said.

✚

"Amputate?" Sunita looks horrified.

It's an hour later. Chico is settled in the recovery room, which has a row of cages in it supplied with extra-comfy blankets. The room is kept warm and quiet, and recovery room patients are checked frequently. There's a clipboard attached to each cage to keep track of information about things like medications and vital signs.

Chico is still very, very weak, and I can tell that Dr. Mac is worried about him. Dad and Sage are on their way home, and Dr. Mac is writing up notes.

I'm not ready to leave, so I join my friends as they clean the reception area of the clinic. I pick up a rag and go through the motions of dusting while I fill everybody in on Chico's status. Sunita's not the only one who's shocked to hear he might lose his leg.

"I can't believe it!" Zoe says.

"I can't believe it, either," I echo.

"Poor Chico. It doesn't have to be the end of the world, though," Maggie says, trying to cheer us up. "Last year Gran had this patient, an Airedale named Buck. His paw was broken really badly when he was hit by a car, and she had to amputate. That dog was up and walking around, like, ten hours after the surgery! And now when he comes in, it's like he always had three legs. You should see him chase after a ball or a stick. Buck runs just as fast as any other dog."

"Still," David says, leaning on his broom, "it's awful. But at least he's not a horse. Horses have to be put down if they break an ankle and the bone can't be repaired."

David is our resident horse expert. He spends as much time over at Quinn's stables, helping to take care of his favorite horse, Trickster, as he does here at the clinic.

"Maybe she won't have to amputate," Zoe says hopefully. She squeezes out her mop. "Maybe he'll be OK." Zoe's always trying to look at the bright side, but even she knows things don't always work out the way you hope they will. One of her favorite dog patients died of cancer a few months ago.

"I hope he will be." Sunita strokes Socrates, Gran's fat, rust-colored tabby. He's sleeping on the counter, in the middle of a pile of paperwork that Sunita is trying to organize.

Sunita has bonded with that cat, big-time. According to Maggie, Socrates has never let anyone else get as close to him as Sunita is. He must sense what a huge cat lover she is. "I wonder where Chico's owners are," Sunita adds. "They must be worried about him."

"Dr. Mac says we should get to work on that," I tell her. "We're supposed to call the shelter and the police and let them know he's here, in case somebody is looking for him. I said I would make some signs, too."

"I'll help," Sunita offers.

"We can all help," Maggie says. She looks around. "I think we're done here, anyway. Let's go into the house and work on signs right now."

"I'll make popcorn for everyone." Zoe loves to feed people. "I think a snack might make us all feel better."

She means well, but I know it's going to take a lot more than popcorn for my mood to improve. It's been a long, hard day, and Chico's life—or at least his leg—is still in danger.

FOUR

I know we shouldn't be doing this. Dr. Mac and my parents would be furious if they knew. But I can't help myself. I'm too furious *not* to do it. Maggie feels the same way. She was really upset and angry about what happened to Chico.

That's why we're here in the woods, hiding behind a boulder. Maggie and I talked about it at lunch today at school, and we agreed. We have to find the creep who set the trap that caught Chico.

It was easy to sneak out of the house. Mom's at work, Dad is in his shop, Jayvee is at soccer, and Sage is at an Animals Always meeting.

Our boulder is about twenty paces from the apple tree where I found Chico. Maggie and I aren't talking much. In fact, we're barely breathing. I feel like a detective on a stakeout, waiting for the criminal to return to the scene of the crime.

I check my camera to make sure that it's ready to shoot. The cut chain is still exactly where we left it yesterday, which means the trapper probably hasn't been by here yet.

That makes me even more mad. Dr. Mac told me that trappers are supposed to check their traps at least once every twenty-four hours. It's the law. If they check regularly, at least the animals they catch won't suffer too long. But Chico's trapper hasn't bothered to care about that. He hasn't bothered to check his traps in much, much longer than twenty-four hours.

My guess is that he'll be along soon.

The skies are gray and dreary, and it's a little chilly. My legs are stiff from sitting in one position for too long. I shift my feet, trying to get comfortable. "Ouch," I say out loud as my muscles protest. A few good yoga stretches would sure feel great right about now.

"Shhh," Maggie says.

I pull my jacket closer around me and adjust my fleece hat so that it covers my ears. We're lucky it wasn't this cold when Chico was caught in the trap. He might have died of hypothermia. Dr. Mac told me she's seen that happen to animals who are outside in the cold for too long. Their bodies lose the ability to fight the cold, their temperature drops, and they die.

I shiver just thinking about it.

I wonder how Chico is doing. I'm keeping my fingers crossed that Dr. Mac won't have to amputate. I can hardly stand the thought of Chico losing his leg, even if what Maggie says is true about dogs being able to adapt.

It's frustrating to have to sit here quietly, doing nothing, when there's so much on my mind. I think of what my mom would say. *Live in the moment, Brenna. Listen to the world around you and let your mind go quiet.*

I take a deep breath and make myself very still. Instead of paying attention to my thoughts, I start paying attention to what's around me.

It works—I feel more relaxed. A blue jay screeches in a nearby tree, and a squirrel chirrups back at the bird, telling it to mind its own business. Three different kinds of moss are growing on the rock near my face, and I spot a snail crawling over a leaf. I point it out to Maggie, and she smiles.

Her smile freezes. We both hear it at the same time: footsteps.

Somebody is stomping through the woods. And there's absolutely no doubt that the somebody is human. A human who is whistling cheerfully and crunching along.

This person has some nerve!

We hunker down even smaller and make sure we're well hidden. Then we peek around our rock, just in time to see the whistler arrive in the clearing.

It's a man—no, a teenager, maybe a little older than Sage. He's dressed in jeans and a red wool jacket, and he's wearing big black boots. That explains the stomping noises. I can't see his face too well, but he's tall and skinny, and his dark blond hair is long enough to peek out from beneath his Yankees baseball cap.

He's still whistling as he strides across the clearing and approaches the apple tree. He bends down to look for his trap. It's not there, of course.

It's in the trash, where it belongs.

He stops whistling. He scratches his head. Then he looks again. He bends over and rustles around in the leaves until he finds the end of the chain that Dad cut. He picks it up and examines it carefully.

He swears out loud. Then he sits back on his heels and stares down at the ground.

I'm getting angrier by the minute.

I flash on the way Chico looked when I first saw him lying there, so exhausted. A dog like Chico should be walking around proudly, his coat gleaming and his tail fluffy. Instead, his coat is matted and the life has gone out of his eyes. He's tired and thin and nearly starving. And he might lose his foot.

What makes this guy think it's OK to kill innocent animals?

I can't take it anymore. I jump up from behind the rock and yell, "If you're wondering where your stupid trap is, I'll tell you. We had to take it off a dog! And the dog might have to have its foot amputated!" My voice sounds funny—high and pinched. I swallow hard to keep from crying.

"Brenna!" Maggie grabs my arm, but I jerk it away and walk toward the guy. "Brenna, please," she says again. "Don't make him mad."

"Don't make *him* mad?" I say.

It only takes me a few seconds to cross the clearing. I stand right in front of the guy, my hands clenched into tight fists at my sides. I'm not sure what to do next. "You, you—" I try to think of a name bad enough to call him.

"Hold on, there," he says, holding up his hands. "Who are you, anyway?"

"I'm Brenna Lake." Now my voice is shaking. "And you know what? This land is a nature preserve. It's illegal to trap here. But you shouldn't trap anywhere, because it's just plain wrong!"

"Look," he says. Now that I'm closer, I can see his face a little better. He has a few hairs on his upper lip, not quite enough to be called a mustache, and some pimples on his forehead. His eyes are light brown. He looks annoyed. "I grew up around here," he says. "My dad did, too. And his dad. We Morrisons have always trapped on this land. It's a family tradition. Don't you be telling me what to do, you little brat!"

I take a step back. He's really angry, and I'm a little scared. Then Maggie yells from behind the rock.

"Brenna!" she shouts. "He's got a gun!"

I glance at his belt, and, sure enough, there's a pistol hanging there in a brown leather holster.

"Listen, you don't understand—" the guy begins.

But Maggie and I aren't listening. We're running as fast as we can, away from the guy with the gun.

FIVE

We run all the way back to my house, crashing through the underbrush. We follow the same route I took when I found Chico. But this time I'm looking over my shoulder every few seconds, half expecting that Morrison guy to be following us.

Maggie's doing the same thing. Out of the corner of my eye I see her stumble and nearly fall, but she manages to catch herself and we run faster. My camera thumps against my chest. I never even took a picture. Doesn't matter. I won't ever forget that guy's face.

Exhausted, we emerge into my backyard. Home safe. I bend over, hands on knees, and try to catch my breath. Maggie flops down on the ground next to me.

"Whew! And I thought I was in shape," she says.

"What are we going to do?" I ask.

"What do you mean, what are we going to do?" Maggie stares up at me. "We're going to stay far, far away from that place, that's what we're going to do. And we're going to hope that guy doesn't remember your name and decide to come calling."

I shudder. Why did I have to lose my temper? When will I learn to keep my mouth shut? "Do you think we should tell my dad?" I ask.

Maggie looks over at the carpentry shop. We can both hear the whine of a saw. "No, he's busy. And it'll only make him worry. We should tell someone, though." She glances down at her watch. "Oh, man!" she moans. "Look how late it is. Speaking of worrying, Gran will be wondering why we're not at the clinic."

"Let's bike over there," I suggest. "Take Sage's bike. He never uses it anymore."

"Good idea," she says. She jumps to her feet and we head to the garage to grab the bikes.

I glance once more at my dad's shop. Maggie's right. He's so busy these days—it's better not to bother him. We push the bikes to the end of our dirt driveway and ride off.

It's only a few miles to the clinic, but the ride gives me a chance to do some thinking.

"I'm going to call the cops," I tell Maggie, as we

wheel the bikes into the garage behind the clinic. "That guy shouldn't be trapping in the nature preserve. Let's have the authorities deal with it." I've decided to be mature about this, do the right thing.

She hesitates, then nods. "OK. Let's do it right now, before we go into the clinic. We can call in private from my kitchen." Maggie's house, where she lives with Dr. Mac and Zoe, is attached to the clinic.

We head straight to the phone. Maggie opens a drawer and pulls out a phone book. "I think you should try the sheriff," she says, leafing through the book to find the number. "He's the one who helped us catch that guy running the puppy mill, remember? And I think that's who Gran calls if she gets a tip about somebody poaching deer."

Poaching deer means hunting deer out of season. You can get in a lot of trouble for that.

I pick up the phone and dial the number Maggie reads out.

"Sheriff's department," says the woman on the other end. "How can I help you?"

"I want to report a crime," I say.

"Hold on." There's a rustling noise, as if she's getting a piece of paper. "OK, go ahead."

"It's about somebody trapping illegally."

"Trapping?" she asks. "We don't deal with that,

hon. Try over at the Game Commission." She gives me the number, and I thank her. My palms are sweaty as I dial again.

"Pennsylvania Game Commission." This time it's a male voice.

"I—I want to report somebody for trapping illegally," I say.

"Hold for the game warden," the guy says and puts me on hold before I can say a word.

"I'm on hold," I tell Maggie.

She rolls her eyes. "This isn't so easy," she says. She grabs a box of crackers from a cabinet, opens it, and offers one to me.

I shake my head. "No, thanks." I don't want to have my mouth full of food when it's time to talk again.

"Hello? Connor speaking. May I help you?"

"Are you the warden?" I ask.

"That's right."

I take a deep breath. Maggie nods encouragingly at me. "Well, I want to report someone for illegal trapping."

"Go on," he says.

"I don't know his full name," I start. *Collect your thoughts, Brenna. Try to sound like you know what you're talking about.* I stop and start over again.

"His last name is Morrison and he looks like he's about eighteen. He's been trapping in the Gold Hill Nature Preserve. He says he's from around here."

Maggie waves to get my attention, then makes her hand into a pistol shape. "Tell him about the gun," she mouths.

I nod. "He had a gun with him. A pistol."

There's a pause. I figure Connor (is that his first name, or his last?) is writing all this stuff down.

"OK," he says. "Anything else?"

"Um, yeah. He didn't check his traps. A dog got caught in one of them and we took him to the vet. He might have to have his leg amputated."

"That's a shame," says Connor. "Thanks for the tip. I'll look into it."

"Please do it soon, OK?" I ask. "Before any more animals are hurt." They've got to arrest this guy and put him in jail.

Connor takes down my name and address.

I hang up with relief. "Let's go check on Chico."

"You read my mind," Maggie says. She leads the way into the clinic.

"Where have you been?" Sunita asks as we walk in. She's at the reception desk again, still trying to sort out the mess of paperwork.

"We found the trapper!" I blurt out. "The one

who caught Chico. We know who he is. He's just a kid, but he had a—"

Maggie pokes me just in time. I know exactly what that poke means, and I shut my mouth fast. It's probably better not to tell our friends and family about the gun. They'd just freak out.

"A what?" asks Sunita.

"A Yankees baseball cap," Maggie says, covering my mistake smoothly. Then, quickly, before Sunita can get suspicious, Maggie changes the subject. "Is Gran mad? Did she notice we weren't here?"

"I don't think so, but—" Sunita stops and frowns. "I'll let her tell you. She's in the operating room."

My stomach does a flip. Whatever the news is, it can't be good. I can tell from Sunita's face.

"Where are David and Zoe?" I ask.

"David's at the stable today. And I think Zoe's in the yard, walking a couple of dogs that are boarding here." Sunita busily shuffles a stack of papers, trying to avoid our eyes.

I look at Maggie. She looks at me.

We head into the operating room, where Dr. Mac is tidying up a shelf of supplies.

"Gran?" Maggie says.

She glances up at us, a little distracted. "Maggie, Brenna," she says. I expect her to ask where we've been, but she doesn't. Instead she comes over to put an arm around me. "I have news."

Her voice is quiet and serious. *Uh-oh.*

"Is it Chico?" I ask. "Did he—?" I can't seem to say the word *die.*

She shakes her head. "He's still here," she says. "But I had to take off that foot."

What's she talking about?

"I had to amputate," she explains. "The surgery went well. He's extremely weak, but I think he's going to make it. My only worry now is that he's not eating. I'm still feeding him through an I.V."

"But—" I feel like crying. I was sure that Chico's foot would heal.

Maggie reaches out and touches my arm. "Can we see him?" she asks her grandmother.

"Sure," Dr. Mac replies. "He's in the recovery room. Be very quiet around him, and keep your distance. As he gets stronger, he's becoming more aggressive. It's not surprising that he doesn't trust people, after all he's been through."

We tiptoe over to Chico's cage. Chico is very still, curled up on his left side with his tail touching his nose. He opens his eyes when he hears us, but he doesn't move a muscle. A huge bandage covers his right shoulder. My jaw drops open.

Chico's whole right leg is completely gone. Just—gone!

I whirl around to glare at Dr. Mac. "Why did you take off his whole leg?" I demand. "Only his foot was hurt!"

"Shhh, keep your voice down, Brenna," Dr. Mac reminds me. "If you take off only the foot, the rest of the leg becomes dead weight to the dog. It'll be much easier for him to get around without any leg at all."

That makes sense, I guess. But still, I can hardly stand to look at the dog. I force myself to step closer to his cage, feeling shaky. "Hey, Chico," I squeak out. "How's it going?"

He can hardly lift his head. But he curls his lip at me and growls.

Chico is mad at the world, and I don't blame him. It hurts, though, that he won't let me get closer. Doesn't he know I'm the one who saved him?

The big white bandage stands out against his dark fur. The look in Chico's eyes makes me want to cry. I think of that Morrison kid. Maybe Sage is right. Maybe jail is too good for this guy.

SIX

Whyat's the point of trapping, anyway? Is it supposed to be fun or something? I don't get it."

It's lunchtime at school the next day, and Maggie and I are still talking about Chico and the trapper. I have lots of questions and no answers.

"Where do you think fur coats come from?" Maggie says. "Trappers, that's where. It's all about money."

She acts tough, but I know how upset she is. Neither of us can stop thinking about the look in Chico's eyes. Or about the leg that was amputated.

David, Sunita, and Zoe are listening in as we finish our lunches. We still haven't told them about the gun, but we told them everything else.

"I thought they came from mink farms, which is bad enough," Zoe says. "My mom used to have a mink jacket. Some movie producer gave it to her."

Zoe's mom is an actress. She's living in L.A., trying to get her career going, which is why Zoe is living with Maggie and Dr. Mac.

"I made her give it away because it grossed me out. I mean, sure, it was super warm. And the fur was so soft! But touching it was like touching a dead animal."

Sunita shudders. "How can people wear something like that?"

"Did you ever hear about those protesters who throw fake blood on models wearing fur?" David asks. "I think that's pretty cool." He points to my apple crisp. "Are you going to eat that?"

I shake my head. I'm not hungry.

He takes the dessert off my tray. "That blood-throwing does make people think," he continues. "I saw a story about it on the news. The protesters got arrested, but I bet it was worth it. I bet they changed some people's minds."

Sage would probably do something like that. He's so angry these days that he'd probably do something even worse. What if he got arrested? What if he got sent to jail?

"There must be something we can do to stop this trapping thing," I say. "Why aren't there any laws against it?"

"I bet we can get some information on the Internet," Sunita suggests. "Want to stay late today and hit the computer lab?"

Of course. I should have thought of that before! I give her a grateful look. "That would be awesome," I say. Then I sneak my hand over and grab the last bite of my apple crisp back from David.

✚

After the last bell rings, we head to the computer lab. "Let's see," Sunita says. She's at the keyboard, and I lean over her shoulder. Maggie, Zoe, and David have all left for the clinic. I'd like to be there, too, but right now this feels important.

Sunita types in some letters. "OK, let's try 'trapping,'" she says, hitting the return button. We wait while the search engine races all over the Internet. I picture a tiny train engine zooming everywhere, hauling a line of cars that fill up to the brim with information. The screen changes, and there's a list of over a thousand matching Web sites. "We have to narrow it down," Sunita says. "What are those traps called again?"

"Leghold traps." I remember Sage saying that.

Sunita nods. "Leghold traps," she types. "Bingo," she says, as another list of topics comes up. "Now we're on the right track." She clicks on an article title, and the screen changes.

It takes a minute for the picture to fill in, but as soon as it does, we both turn away in disgust.

"Ugh!" Sunita cries. "That's horrible! Is that what Chico looked like when you found him?"

At the top of the article there's a picture of a Labrador retriever who was caught in a trap. The trap must have just been taken off. He's lying in the grass, and one of his front legs looks normal. The other is all bloody and gross, and the foot is missing.

Tears spring into my eyes. "Scroll down, scroll down," I tell Sunita. "I don't want to look anymore."

She scrolls down, and we start to read. "This is unbelievable," Sunita comments. "It says here that this kind of trap is already banned in lots of countries and in some states. Why doesn't the United States just ban the traps completely?"

"It sounds like that's what the activists want," I say, reading ahead. "They're working on changing the laws. But I guess change is a long way off. Pennsylvania is one of the biggest trapping states."

I read some more. According to the article, about ten million animals a year worldwide are trapped for their fur. "Man, that's a lot!" I say, pointing to the screen.

"And a lot of them are caught by mistake," adds Sunita, reading quickly now. "This says that for every target animal, like mink or raccoon or fox, two nontarget animals are caught."

"Like Chico," I say softly. I read along with her. Leghold traps catch lots of dogs and cats, plus squirrels, opossums, and even endangered species. Many of these animals die. I sit back, shaking my head in disgust.

We go through a few different articles, and I start to feel sick to my stomach. As Dr. Mac said, sometimes trapped animals die of exposure or starvation. Some are even eaten by other animals, since they can't run away to save themselves. Or they drown if the trap is set underwater. That's pretty common for beavers. And if an animal doesn't die before the trapper gets to it, well, he takes care of that in a hurry. Most trappers shoot the animals, but some trappers actually club them to death, or stomp on them! I know, it's really horrible. Sorry. But it's true.

"So that's why he had a—" Once again, I stop myself just in time. I've suddenly realized why the Morrison guy had a gun. He shoots the animals when he finds them in his traps!

Would he have shot Chico? Or would he have let him go, to deal with his injuries on his own?

"A what?" Sunita asks. She's studying my face. "Brenna, did the guy have a gun?" She's no dummy.

I nod.

She gasps. "Did you tell your parents?"

"Not yet," I admit.

I did tell them about seeing the Morrison kid checking his traps (I sort of made it sound like a coincidence that Maggie and I were there) and about turning him in to the game warden, but that was it. "They'll only worry."

Sunita can understand that. Her parents were really freaked out about her when she was working with some feral cats and was bitten by one of them. She had to have rabies shots! "Just stay out of his way, OK?" she cautions.

"I promise," I say. Right now, I'd be happy if I never saw the guy again. "But it shouldn't be hard. He's probably going to jail."

We read some more articles. "Some people think that trapping isn't always bad," Sunita points out. "Like, some wildlife managers use traps to relocate foxes or coyotes if they're killing off protected bird populations."

"That's different," I say.

"Right, but they couldn't do it if trapping was just plain illegal," Sunita says. "Also, look at this. Other people say that if the traps are padded, they're more humane."

"I don't know," I say. "How can any trap really be humane? The whole thing is just plain wrong." I copy down some addresses. "I'm going to write to these organizations for more information," I say. "Maybe there's something I can do to help."

✚

Later, Sunita and I walk to Wild at Heart. My head is spinning from everything I've learned. We looked at lots of the anti-trapping sites, and even some of the pro-trapping sites. Sunita said that it's important to understand both sides of the issue. She sounds like my mom.

When we get to the clinic, I don't waste any time. I head straight for Chico's cage.

It's empty!

"Where is he?" I demand.

Zoe's there, mopping the floor. "Chico's not in the recovery room anymore," she says. "He's doing much better, so Gran moved him to the boarding kennel."

Sure enough, when I go to the boarding kennel and find Chico in one of the regular cages, he's actually standing up!

"Wow!" I stare at him, keeping my distance. I don't want to scare him.

"Incredible, isn't it?" asks Dr. Mac, coming up behind me. "Dogs adapt so quickly to amputation. It's kind of like nobody ever told them they were supposed to have four legs."

"But how can he balance?" I ask.

She shrugs. "He just does," she says. "He figures it out somehow. Once he gets stronger, he'll be running around in no time."

As if he hears her and remembers how weak he is, Chico lies down and heaves a big sigh. I take a step closer, worried—and he growls, baring his teeth. I step back. Why won't he let me comfort him? I turn to Dr. Mac. "Is he eating yet?" I ask.

She shakes her head. "Unfortunately, no. He doesn't seem to trust any food a person gives him. He'll have to get over that eventually, but for now I'm giving him I.V. nutrition a couple times a day."

"Have you gotten any calls from people missing a dog?" I ask.

"Not a single one," she says. "To be honest, Brenna, I think he may have been a stray for a long time before he got caught in that trap. Judging by the condition of his coat and how thin he was, he's probably been on his own for a while."

Poor Chico. I hope Dr. Mac is wrong and that somebody comes to claim him soon. He deserves a good home, after all he's been through. If he really is a stray, it may not be easy to place him. Who wants a dog who's so mistrustful of people that he growls every time someone comes near?

SEVEN

Something smells good," I say as I walk into our kitchen. Mom is at the counter, chopping up garlic and onions.

She turns to smile at me. Her silver earrings gleam as she moves. The kitchen is warm and welcoming. It feels good to be home.

"I'm making a tofu and veggie stir-fry," she says.

"Yum!" I happen to love tofu, even though everyone makes fun of it. Maybe it's just the way my mom makes it, but I've always thought it was delicious.

Mom turns back to her chopping. "It's easier to cook one thing for everyone," she says. "If Sage wants to be a vegan, we can all try that for a while. I looked up some information on how to make sure we'll get enough protein, and it seems easy enough. There are a lot of good vegan recipes."

"What about milk and cheese and yogurt?" I ask.

"I'm not quite ready to give all that up," Mom admits. "Plus, it's important food for Jayvee, since he's still growing. So we'll continue to have it in the refrigerator. Sage doesn't have to eat it if he doesn't want to."

That makes sense. And I'm relieved. I'd miss those things, especially ice cream. I hope Mom will still be stocking our freezer with the occasional pint of Ben and Jerry's.

"Honey, would you set the table?" she asks. "By the time you're done, I'll be finished chopping the veggies and we can go out and feed the critters." She takes some tofu out of the fridge and starts to cut it up.

I'm thinking that it's Sage's turn to set the table, but it doesn't seem worth arguing about. "Sure," I say, pulling open a drawer to get napkins.

When the table's all ready and the tofu and veggies are chopped, Mom and I head out to the critter barn. It's quiet out there, and we go about our tasks without talking or making much noise.

"Sorry I never got you any treats," I whisper to the raccoon as I dish out some cat food for him and refill his water dish. I feel bad about that. This business with the trapper seems to be taking up all my attention lately.

The raccoon doesn't mind, of course. He barely notices me. And that doesn't bother me in the least. It's funny how much I mind about Chico growling at me. Why shouldn't he? He's in pain. Maybe if I thought of him the same way I thought of our critter barn guests, my feelings wouldn't get so hurt.

On our way back to the house, we stop to tell Dad that dinner's almost ready.

The shop looks even more chaotic than ever. I think Dad's really missing the help that Sage used to give him.

Jayvee runs into the kitchen after we come in. "I'm starving!" he shouts. "When are we eating?"

"Any minute," says my mom, tossing the tofu and veggies into the sizzling wok. "Go tell your brother."

Dinner starts off quietly enough. Everybody's hungry, and we pay most of our attention to the food. The stir-fry is yummy. Then, after I've started in on my second helping, I start to tell a little about what I've learned about leghold traps.

Mom and Dad are nodding. They must know all this stuff already.

Sage keeps chiming in with statistics and gory details. He and the other Animals Always people do a lot of research into this type of thing. They try to write at least one letter to the editor every week, and each one is full of facts and figures about the ways humans abuse animals.

"Ugh," Jayvee says when I tell about how the beavers drown in their traps. "Do we have to talk about this at dinner?"

"Why talk about it at all?" Sage asks. "Talk never changes anything. Direct action is the only way." He's frowning as he toys with his food.

"What kind of direct action?" Dad asks, putting down his fork.

Sage just shrugs. He won't meet Dad's eyes.

"Sage, that group of yours isn't considering doing anything illegal, is it?" Mom asks. She pushes her plate away, looking worried. "I've read about some of the things that the more radical animal rights groups do. Recently they set fire to a factory that makes food for mink farms. That's dangerous! People could get hurt."

"They always make sure there are no people in the building," Sage says defensively.

Mom sighs.

"Why don't they just let all the minks out of their cages?" Jayvee asks.

His innocent question makes Sage grin, and I realize how much I've missed my brother's smile.

"They do!" Sage says. "Isn't that the coolest? They sneak into mink farms at night, all dressed in black. They open up all the cages and liberate the animals! There are directions on the Internet about how to do it."

"Wow, cool . . ." says Jayvee. He pauses. "What's 'liberate'?"

"It means they set them free," my dad explains. He's shaking his head. "And it's not always the best thing for them. Sometimes they run off and get hit by cars or eaten by other animals."

I guess Sage isn't the only one who's been doing his research!

I look at Sage. Our quiet family dinner has suddenly turned into something else. I feel as if I'm at a tennis match, turning my head from side to side as each player hits the ball. Dad, one. Sage, zip.

"Right," Sage admits. "So some of them die. But guess what? If they stayed prisoners at the mink farm, all of them would die." Score one for Sage. "Anyway, usually the people who free them try to catch them and give them good, safe homes."

Dad just shakes his head again. "I'm glad that you care about animals, Sage. We brought you up to respect all living things. I just hope you'll keep in mind that humans fall into that category."

I'm not sure what Dad is getting at, but Sage seems to understand. "Uh-huh," he says shortly. Then he stands up. "I have a meeting to go to," he announces. He takes his plate to the sink and rinses it off. Then, before we know it, he's gone.

"Dessert, anyone?" Mom asks, trying to salvage what's left of our family dinner. "It's apple pie."

✚

After pie, I help Dad with the dishes and then head up to my room to do some homework. I've fallen behind a little, and if I don't study for tomorrow's math test, I could be in big trouble.

When I open my backpack and look things over, I realize that the situation is worse than I thought. I have an English paper due in two days, my social studies group project is supposed to be well under way, and I'm scheduled to give an oral presentation in tomorrow's health class, on food safety.

Eek.

First things first. I'd better get going on that oral presentation. There's only one problem: I left my health book in my locker at school.

If Sage were home, I'd ask him if I could use his computer for a while to do some research on the Internet. (The family computer is way too pokey.)

Come to think of it, if Sage were home, I'd never have a chance at the computer, since he's always using it.

It only takes me a second to decide. He hates me to go into his room without asking, but I don't really have a choice, do I?

I go down the hall to Sage's room and knock softly on the door, just in case he's still there. "Sage?" I call. No answer. I push the door open.

His room looks the same as always, which is to say it's a total pigsty. No, that's not fair to pigs. They're actually very smart and clean. Sage's room is, well, what can I say? I have to practically wade through piles of dirty clothes, books, and wood-working projects in order to get to his desk.

The computer's on, so it only takes me a few minutes to get onto the Internet. I do some searching, trying to remember Sunita's techniques. It's not too hard to find what I'm looking for, and soon I've downloaded more information than I'll ever need about salmonella bacteria counts, hand washing, and how to clean your kitchen counters.

While the information is printing out, I quickly check my e-mail. Nada. Just a couple of those stupid chain letters everybody loves to forward. Then, bored, I do something I know isn't quite right. I go to Sage's list of bookmarks to see what Web sites he's been visiting.

And boy, do I get an education!

These animal rights people are serious. Like that fire my mom talked about, in the feed factory? That was only one of dozens of fires people have set. They've also defaced the windows of stores that sell fur, vandalized fast food places that serve meat, and sent threatening letters to scientists who use animals for experiments.

Some of the people have been arrested for their activities—including some Animals Always members! They're known as "political prisoners," and there's a list of addresses so you can write to these people in jail.

There's a page that shows how to disguise yourself when you're doing "direct actions," and a page that tells how to disable video surveillance cameras so that you can't be filmed while you're freeing minks or setting fires.

No wonder Mom and Dad are so worried about Sage. He could be headed for real trouble if he gets too involved with these groups!

Then, I check one last page. "Directions for Building a Man-Trap," it's titled. There are pictures with captions explaining how to construct a trap that will grab a man's ankle the same way much smaller traps grab an animal's leg.

"Oh, no," I breathe. I think of the way Sage has been talking about "direct action." Is this what he has in mind for the Morrison guy? It can't be. I don't blame Sage for being angry at the trapper who caused Chico's injuries, but my brother would never hurt somebody just to prove a point.

Would he?

Suddenly, I remember the mess that I waded through to get to Sage's desk. I whirl around in the chair and stare at the floor. Woodworking project? Why would Sage be doing woodworking in his room when he can use Dad's shop and all his tools anytime he wants?

I fall to my knees and push aside clothing and books, exposing Sage's project.

It's not a woodworking project at all, though there are a few pieces of wood involved. Mostly, it's made out of metal. And sure enough, it looks just like the trap on the computer screen. The jaws aren't quite like the ones that hurt Chico so badly. In fact, they're padded the way "humane" traps are supposed to be. But they're huge. I wince at the thought of how they would feel clamping down on my ankle.

I sit there, staring at the jumble of metal and wood and shaking my head. *You've gone too far, Sage.* I hate the thought of what that Morrison kid did to Chico, and I hated the sight of the guy when I saw him. I might even have wished that he were the one in the trap—but still, I don't think I could do something like that to another person. If it's wrong to hurt animals, isn't it wrong to hurt humans?

I try to collect my thoughts, figure out what to do. Should I tell Mom or Dad? Confront Sage? Call the police?

None of those seem right. I don't want to get Sage in trouble—and I don't want him angry at me, either. Not if this is how he acts when he's angry!

Instead, almost without thinking, I reach down and—carefully—unhook one of the huge springs that controls the action of the jaws. A spring that size cannot have been easy to find in the local hardware store. Sage must have ordered it specially, maybe even from a trapping supply store.

After I remove the spring, I shove the clothes and books back into what I hope is close to their original position. If I'm lucky, Sage won't notice right away that the spring is missing. That will give me some time to figure out what to do next.

EIGHT

It's hard to sleep. I toss and turn and worry about whether Sage will notice the broken trap, whether he'll be able to fix it, whether I should tell Mom and Dad . . .

The only thought that finally calms me down is that the Morrison kid must be in jail by now. I know, it's kind of weird, but at least I don't have to worry about him being caught in Sage's trap.

At breakfast the next morning, Mom notices how bleary-eyed I look. She puts her hand on my forehead as I'm slicing a banana into my oatmeal. "Are you feeling all right, Brenna?" she asks.

"I'm fine," I tell her.

I glance at Sage, who's staring down into his bowl of granola. He ignores me. Good. At least that means he's not furious with me, which means he probably hasn't noticed the missing spring. Yet.

"Are you sure?" Mom asks, concern in her eyes.

"Absolutely," I say. To avoid any further conversation, I pick up the Local section of the newspaper and glance through the news while I eat. Not much happens in our town. There's a report on a zoning board meeting, and an article about upcoming changes in the sewer system. Talk about excitement! I sigh and start to fold the section up again.

Then a boxed item catches my eye.

"Court News," it's headlined. There's a list of names, and after each one it tells where the people live, what crime they committed, and what happened when they appeared in court. The name "Morrison" practically jumps out at me.

I take a closer look. "Morrison, William, 24 Maple Avenue. Illegal trapping. Fined and released on conditions."

Fined and released! I stare at the words on the page. "No way!" I say out loud.

"What?" asks Dad.

Oops. Maybe it would be better not to bring up this whole subject, not while Sage is at the table. "Oh, nothing," I say. "I just can't believe it would cost so much for a new sewer system in town."

Dad gives me a curious look. "You're interested in sewer systems?" he asks.

"Sure, why not?" I say. Then I take the last bite of oatmeal, jump up, and bring my dish to the sink. Hoping nobody notices, I take the paper with me as I dash upstairs to brush my teeth.

That little blurb in the paper means the Morrison kid—William—isn't in jail after all. That's bad for two reasons. First, he's getting away with what he did to Chico. Second, it's only a matter of time before Sage finds out that I broke that "man-trap" of his, and then just a little while longer before he figures out how to fix it.

Oh, and there's a third reason—the worst thing of all. If Morrison isn't in jail, that means he could still be trapping. More animals could get hurt.

I need to do something.

But what? I sure don't like the way Sage is dealing with the problem.

I look again at the blurb in the paper. It includes Morrison's full name and address. That's it! I'll go to his house and talk to him. Explain why it's illegal to set traps in the nature preserve and wrong to kill animals for their fur in the first place. I'll persuade him to stop.

I can't see a thing wrong with my plan.

✚

"Are you out of your mind?" David stares at me, forgetting all about the piece of chocolate cake on the plate in front of him.

It's lunchtime at school, and I've just told my friends what I'm planning to do.

I see Maggie and Sunita exchanging a look. "It's too dangerous," Sunita says. She must be thinking about the Morrison guy's gun.

"She's right," agrees Zoe. "You can't go to his house. That's nuts!"

"But it's the only thing to do," I insist. "The court didn't take care of the problem, so it's up to me to try to change his mind." I haven't mentioned Sage's trap. The fewer the people who know about that, the better.

"I'm going with you," David says quietly.

"What?"

He shrugs. "If you really feel like you have to go to this guy's house, you shouldn't go alone. So I'm coming."

"So am I," Maggie declares. "After all, I'm the one who went with you to meet him the first time. Might as well finish what I started."

That's that. There's no changing their minds. And secretly? I'm relieved. I was pretty nervous about going by myself.

+

David figures out which bus we should take to get to Maple Avenue. That neighborhood isn't far, even though the kids who live there go to another school. It's just on the other side of the nature preserve from my house. A half-hour walk through the woods would get me to it. I trick-or-treated there on Halloween once.

We walk down the street, checking house numbers. "Here's Eleven," Maggie says.

The next house is Thirteen. "We're going the right way," I say. We keep walking.

"It'll be on the other side of the street," David tells us.

"How do you know?" Maggie asks.

"Because twenty-four is an even number. Eleven and Thirteen were on the right side, so that means the right side is odd numbers. Twenty-four will be on the left."

She shrugs. "If you say so." Maggie's not real good with numbers—unless she's talking about basketball scores.

"This is it," says David, stopping in front of a small white house with green shutters. It's set back a little from the road.

"Yep," I say, checking the name on the mailbox. "This is it, all right."

I look the house over. It's not at all fancy, but it looks . . . well, cared for. The paint isn't fresh, but there are nice curtains at the windows. The lawn is mowed. There's a rusty swing set in the side yard, and a tire swing hangs from a huge old apple tree. There's also a rope ladder hanging down from the tree, and my eyes follow it upward.

"Wow," I breathe. "Nice tree house."

I have a tree house in my yard, too. My dad and Sage and I built it together. It's an excellent place to spend a summer afternoon, reading and listening to the wind in the branches. Poe loves to ride on my shoulder as I climb up, and he hates to leave once we're there. I think he knows it's his only chance for being up high, now that he'll never fly again.

Anyway, the Morrisons' treehouse is even nicer than ours. It's got an actual Plexiglas window and a tiny balcony with a nice railing. Somebody knew what they were doing!

"Well?" David asks. "What do we do next?"

"I guess we knock on the door," I say, gulping a little as I look back at the house. Considering how I behaved the first time we met, jumping out from behind a boulder and yelling at him, I wouldn't blame William Morrison if he slammed the door in my face.

I lead the way up the front walk. There are three steps up to a small porch, which holds several wooden chairs made with tree branches, cleverly bent and tied with grapevines. Cool! Dad would be impressed.

There's a doorbell to the right of the front door, and I reach up and push it. I can hear the ringing inside, and I strain to hear footsteps coming to answer it.

But I don't hear a sound. I ring again. I'm almost starting to hope the guy isn't home. Suddenly, my plan to talk him out of trapping seems a little nuts.

"Wait, what's that?" Maggie asks, turning around quickly.

"I don't hear anything," I say, still listening for footsteps inside.

"No, it's coming from around back. It sounds like somebody talking."

I turn away from the door to listen. Sure enough, I hear a male voice. I look at David and Maggie. They look at me.

"Let's go see," I say, squaring my shoulders.

We go around the house, and there's my old pal William Morrison standing beneath a fir tree along the edge of his backyard. He's talking out loud to something at his feet.

"Calm down, will you?" he asks. "Be still. I don't want to hurt you any more than I have to."

I can't see who—or what—he's talking to until we get closer. Then, suddenly, I can see all too well.

It's a fawn. Not a baby with spots, but a young deer, light brown with a velvety black nose and huge dark eyes.

It's lying on the ground with its bony, lanky legs all twisted beneath it. The fawn is struggling as it looks up at William Morrison, and there's something unmistakable in its eyes.

Fear.

William Morrison is holding his pistol. He's aiming it at the deer. He's getting ready to shoot.

"NO!" I yell.

"STOP!" yells David.

William Morrison turns to look at us. "Hey, what the—?" he begins.

"Don't shoot that fawn," I beg. "Please, please, don't shoot that fawn."

The arm holding the pistol drops to his side. He peers at me, recognizes me. "You!" he says.

"I don't care what you think of me," I say. "Just don't shoot that fawn."

He's still holding the pistol. Now he looks down at it and frowns. "I don't want to," he says, "but she's suffering. Can't you see? Her leg is broken. A fawn this old won't recover from a broken leg." The fawn is lying back now, eyes closed. I can see its ribs rising and falling as it pants. "And she's all torn up from being caught in the barbed wire that runs along our property," continues William. "I guess she managed to free herself somehow, but she's not going any farther than right here."

"I bet Gran could do something," Maggie suggests in a low voice.

"I know she'll at least try," I answer. I turn to William. "Do you have a car?"

He shakes his head. "No—I mean, my mom does, but she's at work."

I nod. "Can I use your phone?"

He looks a little surprised. "Sure, I guess." He gazes down at the fawn again. "Do you know somebody who can help?"

"I think I might," I tell him.

He leads me inside to the kitchen, which is clean and bright. First things first: we'll need a ride to the clinic. I dial my home number. It's not easy, because my hands are shaking a little. The phone rings and rings, and finally someone picks up.

"Hello?" It's Sage.

"It's me, Brenna," I say.

He doesn't respond. I have a sinking feeling that he's discovered the missing spring. "Sage, I need help. An injured fawn. Can you get Dad?"

"I'll come," he says right away. "Dad's too busy."

"But—" I'm not sure I want to deal with Sage right now.

"Tell me where you are," he says, ignoring my protest.

I give up and tell him the address.

"I'm on my way," he says. He hangs up before I can say another word.

NINE

As soon as I hang up, I call the clinic to tell Dr. Mac that we're coming in. Then I turn to the Morrison kid. "My brother's coming," I say. "He'll help us bring the fawn to this animal clinic where I volunteer. The vet there is really nice. She'll do her best to save the fawn. If she can save it, then my parents can take care of it until it's ready to go back into the wild. They're wildlife rehabilitators."

"Really?" He looks relieved.

Ha. Little does he know. If Sage figures out that this guy is the trapper who hurt Chico, I don't even want to think about what might happen.

"Do you have an old towel or a blanket we can put over the fawn?" I ask. "It's important to keep her warm since she might be going into shock, and to cover her eyes to help keep her calm."

He nods and disappears down the hall.

I take a second to look around the kitchen. There are photos on the fridge.

One is of William, standing next to a little girl who must be his sister (she looks exactly like a female version of him). Behind them is a woman who must be his mom. There's a beautiful lake in the background, and mountains. Next to the picture there's a note: "Billy, please make sure Katie gets a bath tonight. I'll be working late."

Billy. Somehow that name makes me hate him a little less. The name, plus the fact that he helps out with his little sister.

There's another picture, of a man who looks a lot like Billy. He's holding up a huge fish and grinning at the camera. He must be Billy's dad. I take a step closer to get a better look, and just then Billy comes back into the room. He's carrying an old army blanket and a threadbare orange towel. "Is this your dad?" I ask.

He nods. "Before he got sick," Billy says. "He died last year."

"I'm sorry," I respond automatically, not knowing what else to say.

He shrugs. "We'd better get out there," he says.

David and Maggie are kneeling by the fawn when we go back out. "She's breathing faster,"

David says. "Kind of panting." He looks up at me. "Do you think she'll be OK?"

"Maybe, if we can get her to Dr. Mac in time."

Billy arranges the blanket around the fawn, working very gently and carefully. He lays the towel over the fawn's eyes.

Then we all just sit at a distance and watch, being as quiet as we can.

When Sage arrives, he takes one look at the fawn and shakes his head. "Brenna, I don't know . . ."

"We have to try," I plead with him. "We can't just let her die!"

Finally Sage gives in. "OK." He turns to Billy. "I'm Sage," he says.

"Billy." They shake hands, something Sage would never have done if he knew who Billy was.

"Can you help me carry him over to the truck?" Sage asks Billy.

"Sure. I think she's a female, though. And she's probably a lot stronger than she looks, so we have to be careful. Deer may look cute, but they're still wild animals. Even fawns can be dangerous."

"That's true," Sage agrees and turns to Maggie, David, and me. "You guys better back up. Brenna, go call the warden and let him know what we're doing with the fawn."

That's right—you're supposed to report it to the Game Commission when you find an injured wild animal.

I dash back inside and make the call.

By the time I return, Billy and Sage have lifted the fawn carefully, keeping the blanket and towel wrapped around her. They carry her toward the truck, which Sage has parked out front. The rest of us follow at a safe distance.

On the way to the truck, we pass a small shed, and I notice a row of traps hanging neatly from hooks along one wall. Sage sees them, too. I watch his eyes go from the traps to Billy to me.

Uh-oh.

He's figured it out. But to my relief, he doesn't say anything. I guess he's concentrating on the fawn.

We load the deer into the back of the truck, then all cram into the cab. It's a tight squeeze, but riding with the deer would be too dangerous. We head for the clinic.

On the way there, I ask Billy how he found the fawn. He tells me he had come home from checking his traps and saw a grown doe just standing there in his yard, watching him. When he walked toward her, she turned tail and ran, but he found the fawn near where she'd been standing.

"She'll probably keep coming back to that spot for days," Billy says. "I've seen that happen. When a doe and her fawn get separated, the fawn usually curls up and stays put until its mom comes back. The doe will expect it to be there, waiting for her."

Billy keeps talking about deer and their habits. It's obvious that he knows a lot about animals and how they live. Part of me is impressed. Another part of me feels like screaming at him, *Why do you care? You're an animal killer!*

But this isn't the time or the place for a fight. And I don't want to get Sage all fired up. I can see by the look on his face that he's doing everything he can to contain his anger. He has to concentrate on driving if we want to have a chance of saving the fawn.

✚

When we arrive at the clinic, everybody is waiting for us. Zoe and Sunita watch as we unload the fawn. Maggie whispers to them, telling them who Billy is.

We bring the fawn into the operating room, where Dr. Mac has everything all ready, just as she did when we brought Chico in. Only this time, the lights are dimmer and Dr. Mac is moving even more slowly and carefully than usual.

"A fawn can literally die of fright," she tells us. "So let's be very, very gentle as we transfer her onto the table."

Once the fawn is settled, Dr. Mac asks us all to stand back. "We don't want to overwhelm her," she explains.

She takes a pulse and checks respirations, calls out the numbers, and then gets to work setting up an I.V. "I'm going to give her a very mild sedative," Dr. Mac tells us, "just enough to calm her down so I can examine her." The fawn, which had been struggling, lies still after Dr. Mac gives her the medication.

"Now I can X-ray her legs," Dr. Mac says. She has a portable X-ray machine, about the size of a toaster oven, that's good for situations like this.

"She got caught in a barbed-wire fence," Billy explains.

Dr. Mac nods, tying on a lead apron to protect herself from radiation when she takes the X-ray. "When they get tangled like that, their legs can break. And this fawn is too old for a broken leg to heal. If her leg is broken, not even the Lakes can fix her up enough to go back in the wild."

I look at Billy. He said the exact same thing in his yard! He really does know what he's talking about.

Dr. Mac finishes taking X-rays and goes to develop the film.

"Good news," she reports when she returns a few minutes later. "No fracture."

I sigh with relief, and so does everyone else in the room. "So, you can save her?" I ask.

Dr. Mac pauses. "I hope so," she replies. Then she gives me a stern look. "Brenna, you and Sage should both know better—moving this deer was very dangerous."

Sage, Billy, and I exchange glances. "But she was suffering!" I say.

"It doesn't matter," Dr. Mac replies, shaking her head. "You could have been seriously injured or caused additional harm to the deer. You put your-selves—and the fawn—at risk."

I know she's right. I hang my head apologeti-cally. Still, it's hard for me to feel bad now that the fawn is getting help.

"But . . . she'll be all right?" Billy asks Dr. Mac.

"I'll do my best," she says. She turns her head in my direction. "I'd like to get her to a point where your parents could care for her, Brenna. The ques-tion is how long she's been injured. If it's been a while, her whole system could be compromised from shock. If not, we may be able to clean her wounds, give her some antibiotics, and send her over to your place."

"She wasn't there this morning," Billy reports. "So it can't be more than a few hours."

"That's good to know." Dr. Mac is working on the fawn as she talks, cleaning the nasty wounds made by the barbed wire. She looks more closely at one of the cuts. "This one may need stitches," she murmurs. "Brenna, can you get me a suture kit?"

As I rustle around in the cupboard, I hear Billy and Dr. Mac talking. He tells her how he learned everything about wildlife from his dad.

"It sounds as if you and your father spend a lot of time in the woods," Dr. Mac says.

"Well, my dad's dead," Billy tells her. "But yeah, I love the woods. When I'm there, I kind of feel like my dad is still around." He's silent for a second. "That sounds dumb, doesn't it?"

"Not at all," Dr. Mac answers.

I find a suture kit and bring it over, walking past Sage, who still hasn't said a word. He's standing in a corner of the room, arms folded, just watching. His mouth is in that thin, hard line, and he's glaring at Billy.

Of course, Dr. Mac is treating Billy just like any regular person who's interested in animals. Why shouldn't she? She has no idea he's the trapper who hurt Chico. I feel like I should let her know who Billy is. But how?

Finally, I blurt it out. "Maggie and I met Billy in the woods the other day," I tell her. "He was checking his traps."

Dr. Mac looks up at me, her right eyebrow raised. I give her the tiniest nod. She's got the picture. She's a little shocked, I can tell. Then she looks at Billy. But she doesn't say anything for a moment. Instead, she goes back to working on the fawn.

Nobody says anything for a while. "There," she says finally, throwing one last gauze pad into the trash. "I think she's stable now, and most of her wounds are clean. All we can do now is let her rest and heal." Dr. Mac shoots me a glance. "Brenna, why don't you take Billy to meet Chico? Sage can stay with me in case we need to move the fawn."

Wow. What a great idea! Maybe it will teach Billy a lesson if he sees what his trapping has done. Dr. Mac is brilliant. I nod. "Sure," is all I say.

I lead Billy out of the operating room and down the hall to the room where the boarding cages are. Sunita and Zoe are there, feeding the cats and dogs who are staying with us. "So, how's Chico doing today?" I ask.

"Much better," Zoe says. "But he's still really weak. Dr. Mac is feeding him by I.V. because he won't eat. He's still too scared to trust us."

When Billy and I are standing in front of Chico's cage, I drop the bomb. "This is the dog we found in your trap," I tell him, watching his face for a reaction.

His jaw drops. "Oh, no!" he breathes when he sees Chico's missing leg. He takes a step closer.

I'm secretly hoping that Chico will growl at Billy, maybe even try to bite him. It would serve him right.

But Chico doesn't growl.

Billy seems to know just what to do. Instead of meeting Chico's eyes, Billy looks away from the dog and talks softly in a low, soothing voice. "Poor boy," he says. "I'm so sorry."

Billy raises a hand super slowly and slips a couple fingers through the bars of Chico's cage. Chico lets him.

Sunita notices. Quickly, she crosses the room, grabs a dog biscuit out of a jar, and walks quietly up to Billy. "Try giving him this," she whispers.

Billy offers the biscuit to Chico.

There's a long pause. We hold our breath.

Then Chico sniffs the biscuit. But he still doesn't take it.

Billy continues holding the biscuit patiently. I don't know how he keeps his hands so steady. Mine are shaking like leaves.

Finally, Chico snatches the biscuit and chews hungrily.

I can't believe my eyes. Nobody has gotten this close to Chico without a major warning, much less gotten him to eat right out of their hand. Not even Dr. Mac!

After he's finished the biscuit, Chico lets Billy scratch his head.

I'm amazed.

And more than a little jealous.

TEN

Billy and I head outside to sit on the porch steps. Sage is still inside with Dr. Mac, so now's my chance to talk to Billy alone. I'm still hoping to change his mind about trapping.

"Do you think he's going to be OK?" Billy asks.

"The fawn, or Chico?" I ask.

"Chico." Billy isn't meeting my eyes.

I know what this is about. Billy is feeling guilty, just like I wanted him to. And a part of me is glad. The same part that wants to yell at him.

But I'm feeling something else, too. I'm feeling sorry for Billy.

"I think he'll make it," I say. Then I can't resist adding, "Not that his life will ever be the same, now that he only has three legs."

Billy lets out a sigh, and his head drops onto his hands.

"Billy," I ask, "if you care so much about animals, why do you trap them?"

For a moment, he doesn't look up. Then he clears his throat. "My dad taught me to trap," Billy says. "We spent so much time together in the woods. We were there in every season, in all kinds of weather. Checking our traplines, hiking the trails—stuff like that. My dad taught me everything he knew about plants and animals and the outdoors. He even knew about bugs!" He gives a weird little half-laugh.

"That's cool," I say awkwardly.

"It *was* cool," Billy says. "Everything he taught me, he learned from his dad. So it was like it all got passed down. But now he's dead. My mom's trying hard to take care of me and my sister, but it hasn't been easy for her. Money's tight. Really tight." He swallows hard. "I don't know if you have a little brother or sister, but if you do, imagine having to see him or her go hungry."

I get a quick flash of Jayvee's face, picturing him thin and sad. Ouch.

"My mom needs my help," Billy goes on. "Trapping is the only way I know how to make money." He spreads his hands. "That's it. That's why I do it. Now you know." He gives me a look, half sad, half defiant.

I hesitate. But I have to ask. "So, does that mean you're still going to do it? Even after you saw what happened to Chico?"

He frowns. "That was bad," he admits. "Really bad. I didn't check my trapline for a day because my sister was sick and my mother was working late. Things were so crazy at home that I just . . . forgot. It won't happen again. And I guess I'll have to find another place to set my trapline. I didn't really understand about the nature preserve being totally off-limits. That's a new thing. The warden explained it all, so now I get it."

So, he is going to keep trapping. What is it going to take to make him stop? "Billy," I say carefully. "I've been learning some stuff about trapping. Did you know that more than ten million animals are killed every year for their fur? And that lots of the animals caught in traps are like Chico, animals that the trappers don't even want?"

Billy sort of grunts. Does that mean he already knows all this stuff?

I decide to keep talking. I tell him everything that I learned about trapping and all the harm it does to animals, just like I'd planned to do when I first headed to his house.

He listens. He really does. He nods once in a

while, and a couple of times he rolls his eyes as if he thinks I'm saying something ridiculous. But he doesn't interrupt. Not once.

I bet I have Chico to thank for that. Billy probably feels so guilty about Chico that he figures he owes it to me to hear me out, at least.

Finally, I finish. I can't think of another thing to say. Billy seems to be mulling it all over, staring down at his hands. We just sit there quietly for a moment.

That's when Sage comes out of the clinic. He stops in his tracks when he sees us.

"What are you still doing here?" he asks Billy angrily.

"I just—" Billy stands up quickly and tries to answer. "I—"

But Sage is too mad to let him finish. "You are a sorry excuse for a human being," he says, shaking his head. "You ruined one animal's life, then you almost killed another for no reason."

"I was going to put the fawn out of its misery!" Billy protests. "Stop its suffering!"

"Yeah, right," Sage says. "I think you're just bloodthirsty. You like killing animals, don't you?" Sage is almost shouting now, and his hands are clenched into fists.

"N-no!" Billy says. "It's not like that! I'm not like that, honest!"

"He's not," I tell Sage, trying to calm him down. "Billy and I have been talking. He explained—"

Sage whirls toward me. "You stay out of this," he hisses. "What do you know about it?"

"She knows a lot," Billy says, defending me. "She's been telling me all this stuff about trapping. Stuff I didn't know."

"You didn't know," Sage mimics in a nasty voice. "Oh, you're so innocent, aren't you?"

"No, I—"

But Sage doesn't let him finish. Suddenly, he leaps at Billy, fists flying.

"Sage!" I shout. "No!" I can't believe what I'm seeing. I grab at his shirt, but I can't get hold of him.

Billy's trying to defend himself, but Sage is out of control. He throws Billy to the ground and begins pounding him.

At first, I panic. "Stop it!" I yell. "Stop it, Sage!"

How can this maniac be my brother Sage, the one who never got in a fight before?

"Sage!" I yell at him. "What about being a pacifist? You're letting the Steven Bauers of the world win!" But he doesn't seem to hear me. He just keeps throwing punches.

Billy manages to scramble to his feet, trying to dodge the blows. But Sage doesn't let up. He swings wildly at Billy.

"Sage!" I yell again.

It's obvious that nothing I can say is going to stop my brother. So I jump between him and Billy, grabbing at Sage's arms to stop him from landing any more punches.

It works.

Sort of.

The only problem is that instead of hitting Billy, Sage hits me.

Right in the mouth.

"Ow!" I step back with my hand to my lip, which is already swelling. I can taste blood.

Sage freezes in place. "Oh, no! Brenna, are you all right?" he asks. "I'm so sorry!" He lowers his fists, looking shocked.

Billy sits down on the ground with a thump and a groan.

"Sage Lake!" Dr. Mac shouts, running down off the porch. "How *could* you?" Sunita, Maggie, Zoe, and David are right behind her. They must have heard all the yelling.

Dr. Mac puts her arm around me and leads me back to the steps. "Brenna, are you OK? Sit down here. If you feel faint, put your head between your legs." She touches my face all over, very gently, checking for injuries. Then she gestures for Maggie to come sit next to me while she checks on Billy.

"Are you all right?" Maggie asks me quietly.

I nod. "Just a fat lip, that's all." It sure is fat. I can barely talk.

Billy tells Dr. Mac he's OK, too. But he's holding his arm, and there's dirt all over his face.

"I don't know what's come over you," Dr. Mac says, turning toward Sage. "Your parents would be shocked to see this."

Sage has the decency to look guilty. And a little scared. "Are you going to tell them?" he asks her, ducking his head.

"No," says Dr. Mac.

Sage looks relieved.

"You are," she finishes.

Sage groans and throws up his hands. "Oh, man! I know I lost it a little. But this guy deserves—"

"Violence is never an answer," Dr. Mac cuts in. "Plain and simple. And your sister certainly didn't deserve to get hit." She shakes her head and turns to go back inside. "I'll get Brenna an ice pack for her lip. Then you're going to drive her and Billy both home. Can you do that, Sage? No talking, no fighting, just straight home. Then you can clue your parents in to exactly what kind of day you had."

Sage looks defeated. I know he thinks a lot of Dr. Mac. It must be hard to have her so mad at him. And he absolutely won't meet my eyes.

"And don't forget to tell them they'll have a new guest coming to stay in a couple of days," Dr. Mac says over her shoulder. "It looks like the fawn is going to make it." Then she heads back inside, shepherding my friends along with her.

Maggie turns to look back at me. "Call me," she mouths, holding a pretend phone to her ear.

✚

I climb into the truck first so Billy doesn't have to sit next to Sage. Sage starts the ignition and drives off. Nobody says a single word.

Sage pulls into Billy's driveway, behind a rusty old white car that must be Billy's mom's. Billy opens the door and hops out. He's still holding onto his arm. I roll down my window. "Bye," I say.

"See you," he answers. "And . . . thanks."

I'm not sure what he's thanking me for. The ride? The lecture on the evils of trapping? The fact that I didn't let my big brother beat him to a pulp?

"You're welcome," is all I can think to say.

Sage guns the engine before the words are all the way out of my mouth, and he speeds out of the driveway.

"Sage," I say, as soon as we're back on the road. "What is up with you?"

"Up?" he asks, as if he doesn't know what I'm talking about.

"You never used to be this way." I look out my window, away from his sullen face.

"Well, maybe I am now. Maybe you'll just have to get used to it." I glance over at him and see that he's gripping the steering wheel so hard his knuckles are white.

I refuse to accept his answer. I'm not ready to give up my brother in exchange for this stranger. "Come on, Sage. Billy isn't a monster. He's just—"

"Brenna, you don't get it, do you?" Sage asks. He's staring hard at the road, and he's still gripping the steering wheel. At least he's driving carefully. "All of our lives, we've helped Mom and Dad take care of animals. Healing critters is what our family does. Why would you want to have anything to do with someone who hurts them?"

I'm not sure how to answer. A few days ago, I felt the same way that Sage does toward Billy. But now I feel like I can sort of see Billy's side of the story, and

I think I've helped him see mine. I still don't agree with what trappers do, but violence and revenge aren't the answer. They don't solve the problem, and innocent people (like me!) can get hurt.

Mom is definitely right—things are not always black and white. More like black and blue! But how can I explain all of this to Sage?

He doesn't wait for me to think it through. He pulls into our driveway, parks the truck, and turns to me. "You can't have it both ways, Brenna. Either you're on the side of the animals or you aren't. Which is it going to be? You have to decide." Then he opens his door, gets out, and slams it shut.

He starts to walk away, but then comes back and opens the door again. "Oh, and by the way, I want that spring back," he adds.

When I don't answer, he slams the door again. I watch him stride toward the house. I never knew you could miss somebody so much, even when they were right there in front of you.

I want my brother back.

ELEVEN

Everyone is pretty quiet at dinner that night. I think Mom and Dad are still in shock about the fight. When they heard what happened, they said they needed time to "process" everything before we discussed it together.

And they don't even know yet who Billy is, why Sage got in a fight with him, and what we were doing at the clinic in the first place.

I know I have to tell my parents about going to Billy's house and rescuing the fawn, since the fawn is coming to stay with us. But for the moment, I'm just not ready to talk about it. I pick at my black bean burrito, avoiding Sage's eyes.

He's not looking at me, either.

Jayvee doesn't seem to notice that anything is wrong. He chatters away about his day at school, his upcoming birthday, and his best friend's new hamster. Mom and Dad laugh at his stories, and he loves all the attention.

"OK, buddy," Mom finally says to Jayvee, after we've finished dessert. "Bathtime for you. I'll be up later to read a book with you."

Jayvee heads upstairs.

"Tea?" Dad asks the rest of us, getting up to put the kettle on. He brings mugs, honey, and milk to the table. "It's time to talk." Mom nods in agreement.

Sage looks away. But at least he doesn't get up and storm off like he's been doing lately.

"Brenna, why don't you start?" she asks. "Tell us the whole story, from the beginning."

The beginning seems like a long, long time ago. I can't believe it's only been a few hours since I left school. "We took a fawn to Dr. Mac's today," I say, after a moment. "Sage and I."

"Wait a minute right there," Mom says. "You moved a fawn? On your own?"

"What were you thinking?" Dad interjects. "You know how dangerous that is."

I roll my eyes. Do I have to go through this again? "I know," I say. "I'm sorry. I promise it'll never happen again."

Mom tightens her lips and shakes her head.

Dad looks mad, too. "Well, that explains where

Sage went in such a hurry today." But then his voice softens. "So, does this mean we're going to have a new guest soon at the critter barn?"

"Dr. Mac thinks so," I tell him. "We thought the fawn had a broken leg, but it didn't. Just some barbed-wire cuts."

"And where did you find this fawn?" Mom asks, trying to remain calm.

I take a breath. "I didn't find it," I confess. "Billy did. Billy Morrison. He's the person who set the trap that caught Chico. That's why Sage started the fight with him."

Mom and Dad just nod. "So he called here, looking for help?" Dad asks.

"Not exactly." This is the hard part. "I went to his house."

Mom gasps. "Brenna!"

"I know," I say. "But, really, it wasn't dangerous. I just wanted to talk to him. And it turned out that he'd found this fawn in his yard, so we took it to Dr. Mac. That's the whole story."

"Most of it, anyway," Sage says now. "But you've heard the rest. About how I ended up—you know, hitting Brenna." He glances at me, then looks away.

Poor Sage! He must really be feeling guilty about what he did to me, even if he's still mad that I stuck

96

up for Billy. I want to tell him that my mouth doesn't even hurt that much anymore, that the swelling is going down. That I've forgiven him. But he won't give me the chance.

"Hold on," Dad says. The kettle is whistling. He gets up to make a pot of tea.

"Actually," I say, "I don't think I want any tea. I'm going upstairs, if that's OK. Homework." Sage has a lot of stuff to work out with Mom and Dad, and I have a feeling that he'll have an easier time of it if I'm not there.

Why do I care? Good question. All I can say is that I do. I'll always care about Sage. He's my brother.

"Good luck," I mouth to him as I walk past. I'd hate to be in his shoes right now. Mom and Dad are really disappointed in him. I don't know if they'll tell him he's grounded, or what. It almost doesn't matter. Disappointing my parents is usually punishment enough.

When I get to my room and unload my backpack, I realize that homework is the last thing I feel like doing. Instead, I go out into the hall and get the phone to call Maggie.

It's a relief talking with her. She's been through this whole thing with me, practically, and it helps to go over it all together.

Maggie's glad to hear that my fat lip is already better. She tells me the fawn is doing well. "And Chico's better, too," she says. "He even ate a little of his dinner."

That's good to hear. "It was pretty awesome how he took the biscuit from Billy," I say.

"Billy? What, so now you're best buds with the guy?" she asks.

"Maggie, he's not really that bad. Ask Dr. Mac. He knows all about the woods, and he really does care about animals."

"Right. He cares about trapping them." Maggie is unconvinced.

"He only does it for the money," I say. I can't believe I'm defending Billy Morrison. "If he had another way to help out his family, he'd probably quit trapping."

Did you ever see one of those cartoons where a character suddenly has a lightbulb appear over his head?

Corny, I know. But that's exactly what it feels like. I've just had a major brainstorm. "Maggie, I have to go," I say abruptly.

"What? But—"

"Talk to you tomorrow!" I hang up.

I lie back on my bed to think, my mind racing. As

soon as I hear Sage come upstairs, I make my way back down to the kitchen to talk to Dad.

✚

"Hi."

Billy Morrison looks up from the piece of wood he's sawing. "Hey," he says. He looks back down and starts sawing again.

It's the next day, after school. I've come to the Morrison house again, this time by myself. And with my parents' permission, too. I have something to discuss with Billy, but it's not about trapping.

I'm not surprised that he doesn't seem thrilled to see me, after everything that happened yesterday. "Sorry about my brother," I say.

"That's OK." He's still sawing away. The board he's cutting is laid between two sawhorses in the backyard.

"You made that tree house out front, didn't you?" I ask him.

"Yup."

It's not going to be easy to get him talking. "And the chairs, the ones on the porch, too. Right?"

"What is this, the third degree?" Billy smiles a little to show he's kidding. "Yeah, I made the chairs. Well, my dad and I did. So what?" He stops sawing and faces me, hands on hips. He's wearing the same red wool jacket that he had on the first time I saw him.

"They're cool, that's all. I noticed them when I was here before."

Suddenly, I'm feeling a little awkward. I take off my hat and twist it in my hands. "Listen, Billy. If you had another way to make money, would you quit trapping?"

"Depends," he says. "What exactly did you have in mind?"

✚

"What's *he* doing here?"

I'm back at home, in Sage's room. We're both looking out the window, watching Billy and Dad talk together in front of the woodshop.

Sage is not happy to see Billy.

"Dad's going to give him a job," I say. "It was my idea. Billy promised to quit trapping if this works out. He's a really good woodworker, Sage. And he'd much rather build things than kill things."

I'm babbling a little, but I really, really want Sage to accept this. To understand. Billy is going to be around for a while, and my brother is going to have to deal with it.

Sage nods slowly. Then he surprises me. "Good for you, Brenna," he says. "Good work."

It's exactly what I wanted to hear. I just never thought he'd say it. "But, Sage," I say. "What about 'direct action is the only way'?"

"Getting a trapper a different job seems like one sort of direct action," Sage says, smiling a little. "But the truth is, I've been doing a lot of thinking ever since you mentioned good old Steven Bauer. And ever since I hit you."

Sage bows his head. "I really, really am sorry about that, Brenna," he continues. "Anyway, I think I've gotten a little carried away with all this animal rights stuff. Not that I'll stop going to meetings or anything," he adds quickly. "I still believe in all the goals. And I'm still going to be a vegan. But I have to admit that you proved there's more than one way to make change happen. I guess what I'm saying is that maybe I learned something from my little sister after all."

I'm stunned.

Then Sage turns and digs around under the bed. "I'm getting rid of this," he says, holding up the parts of his man-trap. "So you can keep that spring you stole." He smiles again. "And just so you know, this isn't what most of the Animals Always people are into. The plans for this trap came from one guy who's really radical."

I nod. "Sage," I begin.

Then I realize that I can't think of a thing to say, so I just throw my arms around him. He gives me a huge hug. I've got my brother back.

TWELVE

Another Sunday morning, another yoga session in the sunroom. I move through the postures, enjoying the feeling of the sun warming my muscles as I stretch.

We do the Eagle, balancing on one foot, focusing intensely. Back down on the floor, we do the Pigeon pose, puffing out our chests, and then flow into the Downward Facing Dog. We move through the Cat, hold the Cobra for five long breaths, then relax into the deep stretch of the Frog.

Mom's eyes meet mine. "Finish with a Lion?" she asks, just like last week. I nod happily. We open our eyes wide, stick out our tongues, and growl.

Once again, Jayvee runs in to join us, adding his baby lion growl to ours.

But this week something's different. This week, Dad and Sage are here, too. We sound like a whole pack of lions. We feel like a family again.

Now that Billy is helping my father in the carpentry shop, Dad has more free time. As for Sage, I guess he's decided that maybe he doesn't have "more important things to do" after all—at least not on Sunday mornings.

I gaze around the room, looking into each Lion face in turn. And then I can't hold it in any longer. I burst into giggles. Mom starts laughing, too. Jayvee rolls onto the floor and hoots happily. That makes Sage and Dad crack up.

Soon, the whole room echoes with our laughter.

✚

Later, I ride my bike over to Wild at Heart. I'm really looking forward to spending a regular day there, working with my friends. Things have been so crazy lately! I've missed my usual routine. It'll be a relief to walk in, grab a mop, and start cleaning.

But do I head for the broom closet when I arrive? Of course not. First I have to check up on Chico and the fawn. I've brought my camera, thinking I can take pictures of both of them. A nice picture of Chico might help us place him in a good home.

I head for Chico's cage first, but he's not in it!

For a second, my stomach does a little flip. Did

something go wrong? Then I see Zoe walk in, leading Chico on a leash.

I take the lens cap off my camera and focus on the two of them. *Click.* Chico looks so much better than before. His coat is shinier, his eyes are brighter, and his tail is waving like a flag.

"He's walking?" I ask, even though I can see for myself that he is.

"Well, duh," says Zoe. "Actually, he's doing a lot more than walking. He just chased a squirrel all over the backyard! Almost caught it, too. And he went up and down the stairs without any problems at all. Dr. Mac says that learning how to go down stairs is one of the hardest things for dogs that have lost a front leg. But he did great!" She beams down at Chico but doesn't reach out to pat him. "He's still not the friendliest dog—but who can blame him?" she adds.

I snap another picture as Zoe walks Chico back to his cage. It's just like Dr. Mac said: he doesn't even seem to notice that anything's missing. He's doing just fine on three legs. "So, he's all ready to go home?" I ask.

"If he had a home," Zoe answers. She unclips Chico's leash and lets him back into his cage.

I come closer and we both look in at him.

This time he doesn't growl at me. I get a biscuit from the jar and offer it to him, and he actually takes it!

I guess his attitude has a lot to do with my own. When I was so upset and angry about everything, Chico could probably sense it. He didn't want anything to do with me. But Billy was calm and patient, and that made Chico feel less threatened.

A few days ago, I never would have believed that a hunter could actually be more tuned in to an animal than I was.

Just then, Maggie walks in. "Hey, have you seen the fawn yet?" she asks. "I think she's almost ready to be moved over to your place."

"Cool!" It'll be fun to have the fawn to take care of. Maggie and I go over to the deer's cage, which is set apart from the others and draped with blankets to keep it quiet and dim. I peer in.

The fawn is lying down, but when she hears me, she jumps to her feet. Her cuts are healing beautifully, and it's obvious that all four legs are working just fine. She's gorgeous, with her huge eyes and soft, brown coat.

Moving slowly, I focus my camera and take a few quick shots, hoping there's enough light for them to come out.

"She looks great," I whisper to Maggie.

It's hard to tear ourselves away from the fawn, but there's lots to do. I get to work cleaning cages to make them ready for any boarders we might get this week. It feels wonderful to be scrubbing away without any worries.

"Nice job!" I turn around to see Dr. Mac nodding approvingly. "These cages are gleaming. Thanks, Brenna."

"No problem. Hey, the fawn looks great. Chico does, too."

Dr. Mac smiles at me. "Two success stories," she says. "We can always use those around here."

I look over at Chico's cage. "Well, sort of a success," I reply. "Chico still doesn't have a home. I sure wish I could take him, but there's no way that we can have a dog. Not with all the wild animals at our place."

"Oh, I think I know somebody who may want him," says Dr. Mac, a little mysteriously.

"Who?" Maggie, David, Sunita, and Zoe have joined us by then, and they're just as curious as I am.

"Billy." Dr. Mac beams as she sees five jaws drop. "He came by here yesterday, and we talked about it. He's afraid his mother won't agree because of the expense, but I offered to continue caring for

Chico for free if Billy and his family will give him a home."

Dr. Mac can afford to do things like that. She's made lots of money from some vet instruments she invented, and she also writes a column about animals that runs in newspapers all over the country.

"Really?" says Maggie.

"That's awesome!" I say.

It dawns on me that I have a lot to thank Billy for. If it weren't for him, I never would have learned that not everybody who hunts or traps is evil. And now that I understand why some people trap, I think I'll have a better chance of convincing them not to. (And believe me, I do intend to work hard to ban trapping in this country.)

Even Sage now realizes that by understanding another person's point of view, it's easier to work together for change.

It's kind of like yoga. If you resist stretching, it only hurts worse and your body rebels. But if you give in a little, relax, you can stretch farther than you ever thought you could.

✚

Later that day, Billy and his mom and his sister come by to visit Chico. I feel a ridiculous urge to cry when I see how Chico stands up and wags his tail as soon as he hears Billy's voice.

When they take Chico out of his cage for a walk, I run to find my camera. I make the four of them stand out in back of the clinic, posing for me. *Click.* I take one shot, then another. *Click. Click.* Billy and his mom smile at each other. *Click.* Billy makes rabbit ears in back of his sister's head.

Then, I see it. The perfect shot. All three humans are looking down at their beautiful new dog. Chico looks straight at the camera, chest puffed out proudly. He already belongs with the Morrisons— anybody can see that. He'll be going home soon, and he couldn't ask for a better family to live with.

Click.

I've got the picture. And this time, it's not in black and white.

Animal Rights 101

By J.J. MACKENZIE, D.V.M.

WILD WORLD NEWS—We humans share our planet with an astonishing number of other species. But animals don't always get a fair shake. Since they can't speak for themselves, animals need our help and protection. There are dozens of ways you can get involved in saving their lives or making their lives better. Here are just a few ideas.

Shop Against Cruelty. Make a fashion statement! Avoid buying clothes and accessories made of real fur or wild animal skin. If there's less of a demand for these products, fewer animals will be trapped

for their skins or coats. If you love the look of animal prints, you're still in luck. Fake furs and skins come in lots of fun patterns and colors.

Don't buy jewelry or other objects made from materials that come from endangered species.

Continued on page B8

A Second Chance

Continued from page B6

The African elephant could become extinct because of the demand for ivory.

In an average year, millions of animals are injured or killed during testing of cosmetics, skin care products, and household cleaners. You can help reduce this number by buying only from companies that don't test their products on animals to see if the products are safe for humans. Look for words such as "cruelty free" on the label. You can also have fun making your own cleaning products at home! Look for "recipe" books at the library.

LOOK FOR SOAPS AND SHAMPOOS NOT TESTED ON ANIMALS.

Pet Protection. If your family is thinking about getting a pet, consider bringing one home from your local shelter instead of buying one from a pet store. You won't run the risk of supporting a puppy mill (a place where hundreds of dogs a year are bred in unhealthy conditions just to be sold for profit), and you might be giving a homeless animal a second chance at life.

If your heart is set on a purebred dog or cat, find out about local rescue agencies that match families with purebreds who have lost their homes.

Get your cat or dog "fixed," which means spaying a female or neutering a male. Millions of unwanted kittens and puppies are born every year and end up in shelters or at the pound. If homes aren't found for them, they may be put to death.

Make sure your pet wears an identification tag, even if he or she normally stays inside. Indoor cats who don't know their surroundings can get lost if they accidentally slip out. Keep a sign on your window, in case of fire or other emergency, to alert rescue workers that there's an animal inside who needs their help!

Pitch In, Speak Out.
Volunteer at your local Humane Society. Walk a dog, clean out cat cages, or even be a foster parent for puppies and kittens! Or find out if there's a wildlife rehabilitation center nearby where you can volunteer. Even if

you can't work directly with the animals, you may still be able to help in other ways, such as raising money or doing publicity.

ANIMAL SHELTERS CAN ALWAYS USE A HELPING HAND.

If you see a pet or wild animal that is being abused or neglected, tell an adult immediately. Contact your local ASPCA (The American Society for the Prevention of Cruelty to Animals), Humane Society, or police department.

You can help wild animals by caring more about the environments they live in. Pollution, overpopulation, and the destruction of ecosystems are all contributing to animal extinction. Help clean up a beach, volunteer at a nature center, or start a letter-writing campaign to your local newspapers,

business owners, or members of congress to raise people's awareness and fight for laws that protect wildlife habitats.

Plans to Expand Nature Preserve Approved

About the Author

Laurie Halse Anderson has had many pets—dogs, cats, mice, even salamanders. Her best dog was a German shepherd named Canute. She got him from a shelter when he was two years old. Canute was Laurie's constant running companion. He helped her get into shape for a half-marathon. A few summers ago, he died in her arms. She keeps his collar in her office for inspiration while writing.

Laurie has written many books for kids, including picture books and novels. When she's not writing or teaching writing workshops at local schools, Laurie splits her time between bird-watching and hanging out at the local vet clinic. She lives in Ambler, Pennsylvania, with her husband, her two daughters, and a cat named Mittens.